ELEMENTAL FAE QUEEN

USA TODAY BESTSELLING AUTHORS

LEXI C. FOSS & J.R. THORN

This is a work of fiction. Names, characters, places, and incidents are either the product of the author's imagination or are used fictitiously, and any resemblance to actual persons, living or dead, business establishments, events, or locales is entirely coincidental.

Elemental Fae Queen
Copyright © 2020 Lexi C. Foss & J.R. Thorn
All rights reserved.

No part of this book may be reproduced in any form or by any electronic or mechanical means, including information storage and retrieval systems, without written permission from the author, except for the use of brief quotations in a book review. This book may not be redistributed to others for commercial or noncommercial purposes.

Editing by: Outthink Editing, LLC
Proofreading by: Katie Schmahl
Cover Design: Covers by Juan
Cover Photography: Wander Aguiar
Cover Models: Joli, Pat, Forest, Alex, Camden, & Philippe
Published by: Ninja Newt Publishing
Print Edition
ISBN: 978-1-954183-04-9

ELEMENTAL FAE QUEEN

ELEMENTAL FAE QUEEN

**All I want for Christmas is to feel my legs.
Because my mates broke me.**

After years of adoration and love—and lots of intimacy
—my guys have a special holiday request.

A little fae baby.

Like a fool, I agree, but there's no way I can choose who
gets to be the father. So, my guys have come up with a
solution. A series of trials will determine who'll do the
deed; namely, one in the bedroom that has me
questioning if my lady parts are really up for this. Right
now? Yeah, I can't feel my legs.

Except one look at my mates has me caving. The idea of
them as dads melts me into a puddle of Claire-goo.

Even if their timing can't be worse. My dream of
opening an Interrealm Fae Academy is just within reach.
Then my pregnancy arrives with one hell of a twist.

I'm going to have to count on my guys more than ever to get me through this mess.

Wish my mates luck. They're going to need it. Because a pregnant fae with control over all five elements is a challenge unlike any they've ever faced before.

Something tells me this is going to be one unforgettable holiday.

Author's Note: *Elemental Fae Queen* is a standalone why-choose novel with a happily-ever-after ending. It features characters from the Elemental Fae Academy world but can be read without previous knowledge from the trilogy. This book was previously titled *Elemental Fae Holiday*.

To all the women who have gone through pregnancy, wished their husbands were more helpful, and fantasized about a team of supportive, sexy men. This book is for you.

And to our husbands, for taking care of everything in our lives while we played with fae.

Elemental Fae Queen is a standalone reverse-harem paranormal romance. It focuses on characters from the *Elemental Fae Academy* universe and includes a few cameos from *Midnight Fae Academy* and *Fortune Fae Academy* characters.

While this story contains crossovers within the fae universe, it takes place in the future and doesn't require knowledge of previous books. It also happens after the events in the other series; therefore, this isn't concurrent with those timelines and instead takes place after the conclusion of those stories.

This is a holiday-themed story with steamy scenes, emotional twists, and a little bit of fae politics sprinkled on top. There are also some MMF scenes with emphasis on the MM. Claire's mate-circle has grown rather close over the years ;)

Enjoy!
Lexi & Jen

PART ONE

Trick Or Treat...
Give Us
Something
Good To Eat

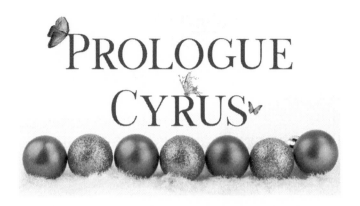

PROLOGUE
CYRUS

SEX WITH CLAIRE was my favorite activity. But there was something innately beautiful about holding her afterward and watching her sleep in this fully gratified state.

I could feel through the bonds that Exos and Titus shared my opinion. Even Vox and Sol were content, though they were elsewhere at the moment, preparing a surprise for our Claire.

Our little half human adored the holidays, and we wanted to make this year extra special for her. We had an ulterior motive, one we all hoped she would enjoy and accept.

A child.

It'd been a conversation whispered about between the mate-circle, but not fully explored. And we wanted to start the preparations for it now.

Which requires our little queen to be in a favorable mood.

Hence the fuck fest Titus, Exos, and I had just provided.

I met my brother's sapphire gaze over her shoulder, his expression knowing. Titus was lost between her legs, his head using her thigh as a pillow. But when I looked

1

down, his dark green irises sparked with embers and excitement.

We had a proposal to make.

One we hoped our mate would accept.

Tomorrow, I thought. *Tomorrow, we'll tell her what we have in mind.*

And then the trials could begin...

CLAIRE

Pumpkins.

My mates carved pumpkins!

I stared at the display in awe, surprised that Sol had allowed Vox to desecrate one of Earth's creations in such a manner. The one and only time I'd mentioned Halloween festivities to him, he'd gone into shock before engaging in a rant about humans having no respect for the earth and its finer qualities.

"First, you cut down trees and decorate their corpses in gaudy strands and ornaments for Winter Festivus, or Christmas— whatever the hell it's called. And now you're telling me they gut pumpkins and take a knife *to the sacred shell? Why in the five sources would anyone do such a thing?"*

And that had effectively ended our discussion on Halloween traditions.

But he stood before me now, holding a big orange jack-o'-lantern.

Vox was beside him with a different sort of creation. His carving resembled a bell shape, making me wonder if he'd confused the Christmas ornaments with Halloween traditions. However, I smiled like a loon anyway.

"They're perfect," I said, delighted by the festive decorations. I wanted something that would bring all the fae realms together today, and this would surely do it. Because we all shared one thing in common—the Human Realm. So why not borrow from some of their fun traditions to set the tone for agreement?

"We have more to show you," Vox murmured, his voice holding a husky note that always made me weak in the knees.

My Air Fae just had a way with sound, something I swore he used the winds around us to highlight. He'd grown even more powerful over the years, his ties to me and the source highlighting his former royal connection and strengthening his bonds to our shared element.

Even now, I could see the power swirling through his long, dark strands. He wasn't wearing his trademark warrior tail today but instead allowing his hair to brush his strong shoulders.

"Yeah." Sol cleared his throat. "We, uh, decorated your office, too."

My eyebrows lifted. "You did?"

They both nodded.

"Want to see?" Vox asked.

"Do we have time?" We were supposed to be heading to the neutral zone in the Human Realm to meet the other fae for the annual Interrealm Fae Council meeting —something that had just been established over the last few years.

"We have two hours," Vox replied. "Plenty of time."

"And it'll be a good distraction," Sol added, his earth gaze knowing.

All my mates could feel the nerves rioting inside me, just as I could sense them all sending calming energy my way. But it wasn't every day I had to deliver a proposal to all of fae kind.

My mates' idea of a distraction was very welcome, so I nodded. "I would like to see it. Just don't let me be late."

Vox snorted, his silver-rimmed black eyes glimmering knowingly. He was never late, a fact he reminded me of with that look.

"Okay, show me," I said, my curiosity piqued.

I'd started adding items to my office around each holiday about two years ago. Just subtle reminders of home. While I loved my fae and their festivities, I often felt nostalgic for the traditions of my past. I grew up with my human grandparents in Ohio, always celebrating Halloween, Thanksgiving, Christmas, and a myriad of other holidays.

Things weren't the same here.

That didn't make them bad.

Just… different.

Sol and Vox set their pumpkins down on the stoop of our Elemental Fae Academy home, then escorted me into the heart of campus, where I kept my office.

Several fae waved along the way, everyone cheerful and pleasant in the autumn weather—weather that also reminded me of home.

Except the trees here didn't change like they did in Ohio. Instead, they remained green, and it never really snowed on Academy grounds. The elements kept everything thriving, indulging in a very different circle of life from the Human Realm.

A hint of nostalgia touched my chest, something that seemed to happen during this season every year. I'd learned to ignore it mostly, but I still dreamt of snowy trees, Christmas lights, and even Santa Claus.

Ridiculous, yes.

But some childhood experiences never died.

"Okay, close your eyes," Vox said as he led me to the door of my office. "No peeking."

"I don't peek," I replied.

"Sure, you don't," Sol drawled, his low timbre a caress to my senses. He came up behind me—his large, muscular body the biggest of all my mates—and grabbed my hips. "Don't think I've forgotten about that time with the blindfold."

"You didn't ask if I could see through it," I reminded him, my insides warming at the memory of Vox and Sol playing with sensory deprivation.

My Earth Fae mate was the rock of our mate-circle, his dominance quiet and strong and oh-so Sol. While Vox was my philosophical, wise mate. He always thought everything through and often provided the voice of reason that I needed.

"Excuses," he grumbled against my ear, his earthy scent wrapping around me in a cloak of comfort. "You knew what we expected from you, little flower. And you cheated."

"I would hardly call it cheating. I would have known who was who regardless." They'd wanted to play a sexual game that required me to guess who was inside me.

Sol's girth always gave him away, just like Vox's long length.

Heck, everything about them was unique. Even their tongues and the way they touched me. Sol always held back, afraid his much-stronger form would crush me, and Vox preferred sensual strokes and wind kisses.

Which, of course, had my thighs clenching. Because now I wanted sex.

And something told me that had been Sol's intent as he aligned his chest to my back and wrapped his arms around my waist. "We'll have to play again to find out," he hummed against my ear.

"But decorations first," Vox insisted. "Now close your eyes, Claire."

A shiver traversed my spine at the demand in his tone, my insides heating all over again with the promise of what was to come.

My mates liked to play.

And I liked to play, too.

I closed my eyes and relaxed into Sol's hold. My pointy ears—something I still wasn't fully used to—twitched as the door swept open. Then my nose picked up on the subtle hints of foliage.

Sol had created something. My affinity for earth roared to life, trying to identify the foreign substance. It wasn't Elemental Fae in origin, but foreign. Not human, either.

My lips curled down as I tried to determine the roots. But then Sol urged me forward with his much-bigger body guiding mine from behind, pushing me into my office.

Lights flickered beyond my closed eyelids, and the door whispered closed behind us.

"Okay," Vox said. "You can look now."

I squinted my eyes first, nervous, then immediately widened them at the sight of my fully transformed office.

A tree stood rooted beside my desk, branches resembling vines along my ceiling and wrapping around the upper molding of my walls. Yellow, red, and orange leaves decorated the limbs, their vibrancy the embodiment of autumn colors. A breeze ran on a loop between them, spreading the fragrance of home throughout my office.

"Oh, it's beaut—"

I jumped as a skeletal thing appeared in the corner, billowing in the wind in a ghostlike state.

My eyes widened. "What the hell is that?"

Vox and Sol followed my gaze, the former frowning and saying, "It's supposed to be a skeleton. Like for Halloween. Exos created it using spirit magic. Did he do it wrong?"

I blinked. "He used...?" I trailed off, because, yes, I could feel it now, the hint of his element weaving through the skeletal structure, commanding it to disappear and reappear at random.

A Halloween trick.

"Oh." I grinned. "That's clever." I took in the tree again. "And this is amazing. What breed is it?" I pressed my palm to the bark, asking it to speak to me, but all it did was whisper Sol's name.

"I, uh, sort of made it up. You once told me about the leaf cycles from home, but ours don't do that. So I created a tree with leaves naturally occurring in your autumn colors. It will always look like this. I guess we can call it an autumn oak?"

"Autumn oak," I repeated, my heart thudding in my chest. "Yes. Oh, Sol, thank you!"

I spun around in his arms to kiss him, only to be caught off guard by the glowing pumpkin lanterns strung around my door. My eyes widened at the very real flames brightening the insides of the hollowed-out baby pumpkins. They were all strung together by strands of water swirling with spirit and air.

"Wow," I breathed, stunned by the gorgeous use of elements.

"You like it?" Vox asked softly, his chest caressing my back as he sandwiched me between him and Sol.

"It was Vox's idea," my earth mate said, a note of annoyance in his tone. "He made me create all those pumpkins just for Titus to gut them."

"And we're making a pie from it all," Vox added, his tone excited. "River gave us a recipe to try. I've already started the process back at home."

"Pumpkin pie." I couldn't hold back the excitement in my voice. "Are we... are we going to have Thanksgiving this year?" We'd never really celebrated it before.

"We're looking into it," Sol replied, reaching up to twirl one of my blonde strands around his finger. "But we want to focus on Halloween first."

"Yes, definitely Halloween," Vox murmured, his lips falling to my neck. "A very memorable Halloween."

My brow furrowed. "What do you mean? The fae don't celebrate Halloween."

"That doesn't mean we can't," my air mate whispered against my ear before nibbling on the lobe. "Do you like your decorations, Claire?"

"I love them." I tried to face him, but his hands landed on my hips, forcing me to remain in place.

Sol's touch drifted from my hair to my cheek, his massive palm cupping my jaw with his trademark tenderness. "Did we get it all right, little flower?"

The ghostly skeleton chose that moment to whisper through the room, disappearing into a wall. My cheeks began to burn from smiling so hard. "It's all perfect," I said, meaning it. "But I don't understand why you did this."

"Can't we do something nice for our mate?" Vox asked, his lips tracing the column of my neck.

"You always do nice things for me," I replied, leaning into Sol's palm and elongating my throat a little more for Vox's mouth.

"Then this shouldn't be a surprise," Vox replied.

"But it's a lot more than we usually do." Last year, I just had a pumpkin on my desk. Then I'd gone a little overboard on Christmas decorations shortly after because I'd needed a little human fix. I intended to do it all over again this year, and being surrounded by autumn remnants now only made me more excited to play with winter-themed ornaments and spice up our homes with holiday cheer.

That was the upside to having multiple places to stay —it gave me that much more to decorate.

"Maybe we want to make this year extra special." Vox's mouth returned to my ear. "Our mate-circle is turning five years old soon."

"Yes," Sol agreed, his earthy gaze following the movement of his thumb as he drew a line across my bottom lip. "Consider this an anniversary gift of sorts."

"An early one," Vox whispered, his tone eliciting a trail of goose bumps along my skin.

I melted into them, their seductive touches lulling me into a sense of peace only my mates could inspire. They were doing this to put me at ease, to ensure I was entirely relaxed for the Interrealm Fae Council meeting.

This was just one of the many reasons why I loved them.

They always knew what I needed, their intuition tied to their abilities to read my thoughts and mine theirs. But I sensed they were hiding something from me now. Some sort of big surprise.

I didn't pry because I wanted to enjoy whatever they had in store for me.

Sol rewarded my acquiescence with a kiss, his tongue sliding in to slowly dominate mine in a thorough and powerful way that was all him.

Vox nipped my shoulder, his hands drawing the fabric of my dress upward, the silk tickling my thighs along the way. "She's not wearing underwear again," he said as he revealed my hips.

"Naughty, Claire," Sol said, then took my mouth once more before I could reply.

You guys keep ripping off my underwear, I said into their minds. *It's much more economical to go commando.*

"Mmm, we're not complaining," Vox said, his palm flattening against my thigh before sliding toward my center.

His touch was always like this—precise and knowing.

Just as Sol maintained his possessive hold, his hand drifting from my cheek to the back of my neck to angle me to more thoroughly receive his kiss.

I lost myself to them, allowing them to guide me into the sensual act our bodies all craved.

Vox slid two fingers into me, his growl hot against my neck. "Fuck, Claire."

"That's exactly what I want you to do," Sol replied, his teeth skimming my lower lip. "I want you to sink balls-deep into her sweet heat while she swallows my cock with this beautiful mouth."

My blood heated with the illustration his crude words provided.

Over the years, Sol had really come into his own, taking charge where he wanted and always offering me the safety and warmth I craved.

He was my literal rock.

I kissed him again, my soul igniting into an inferno of need as Vox added a third finger below.

Sol pawed at my shoulders, dragging the straps of my dress down my arms to my wrists, successfully exposing my braless chest. He made a low noise of approval before palming both of my breasts and giving them a sensual squeeze. I arched into him, moaning his name, then falling into a groan from Vox's stimulation between my legs.

"Oh, Fae," I breathed, trembling from the onslaught of pressure building in my lower belly.

Only, my mates didn't allow me to fall over the edge. Instead, they spun me around to push me down onto my desk, my hard nipples protesting against the wood.

I glanced over my shoulder, a complaint clawing up my throat, only for the words to go dry at the sight of Vox unzipping his black dress pants, his heated gaze on the space between my legs.

His arousal always undid me.

All of my mates had that impact.

Including Sol as he strolled around the desk to unfasten his own pants in front of me. His fingers feathered over my jaw before going to my hair, his brown-green eyes capturing mine to evaluate my acceptance.

Whatever he saw in my features must have confirmed it for him, because his touch shifted back into my hair, where he tangled his grip in my strands. He pulled me just a little bit to the side, lining my face up with his groin, while Vox stepped between my legs from behind.

Thank the Fae for the desk beneath me. It gave me the leverage and sturdiness I needed to make this possible.

"Open your mouth, little flower," Sol said, his tone softer than a true command.

His girth had always proved a challenge for me to

swallow—a challenge I very much enjoyed. Something I allowed him to see now as I held his gaze and moisturized my lips with my tongue.

Vox's palms found my hips, his cock nudging my entrance as Sol slid into my mouth.

Their thrusts were gentle at first, their care for me evident in their steady pace. But as our arousals intensified, their movements grew faster and harder, Sol hitting the back of my throat while Vox slammed into me below.

It was dirty. Hot. *Beautiful.*

My senses were on fire from the surrounding autumn elements, all created by my mates for my personal enjoyment.

Vox breathed air around my stimulated form, his affinity stroking my clit in a breezy kiss that sent my soul soaring toward the clouds. Then Sol grounded me with his shaft, his earthy essence trickling down my throat in a prelude of what was to come.

I moaned and shook between them, overpowered by our connection, our mate-circle throbbing to life inside my heart and caressing each of my nerve endings.

Cyrus, Exos, and Titus were all aware of what was happening right now, and I could feel their collective intrigue. Titus sent fiery kisses to my spirit, reminding me of the hot strokes of his tongue against my clit last night. Cyrus whispered icy thoughts of cold promise, forcing me to recall how he'd used ice to counter Titus's tongue, the dual sensations driving me mad.

And Exos's soul stroked mine, his spiritual being joining Vox's air essence against my sensitive center, causing me to cry out.

All of them were in me, even though it was only Sol and Vox in this room. But I felt us all playing together, climbing higher and higher to a climax that was going to split me in two.

Sol flexed his hips, sending himself even deeper into my throat, forcing me to take more of him. I wrapped my hand around the base, stroking him in time with my mouth.

Vox's palms were brands against my hips, his long length hitting that spot deep inside me that elicited the most-addictive pleasure.

He knew how to angle himself just right, stroking me on repeat and shoving me closer... closer... closer...

I could feel them chasing me, their pleasures mounting in tandem with mine, dancing together on a plane of elemental existence only our mate-circle understood.

And then a wave of power crashed through us all, Cyrus sending a sensual push that threw all three of us over the cliff together into an oblivion underlined in passion and love.

Sol ground out a curse, Cyrus's name on his tongue.

Vox groaned.

And I screamed around the shaft unloading down my throat.

It was intense and overwhelming and perfect, leaving me in a cloud of delirium I never wanted to surface from.

I swallowed everything Sol gave me. Squeezed every drop from Vox between my legs. And all but collapsed onto my desk.

The earthy scent of the autumn leaves provided a sweet stroke across my existence, alighting me from the inside out and leaving me blissfully pleased between my two mates.

Vox bent to kiss my shoulder, and Sol brushed his

knuckles across my cheek as he carefully dislodged himself from my mouth.

I need a nap, I thought at them.

They both chuckled in reply, then Sol went to his knees before me to press his nose to mine. "You can nap on our way to the Human Realm. I'll carry you."

I started to nod, my eyes falling closed.

Then I remembered what I had to do when we got there and groaned—a sound that turned into a pleasant moan as Vox slipped out from between my legs. Every part of me tingled in reply, my body already preparing to go again.

Years of satisfying five mates had preconditioned me to accept multiple orgasms.

Not a bad life.

But it definitely became problematic when on a timetable such as this because there was no time for more sex.

You're insatiable, little queen, Cyrus mused into my thoughts.

Stop reading my mind, I replied.

We're reading your spirit, Exos corrected. *You're practically writhing in the spirit realm, begging to be fucked again.*

I wonder why that is, I shot back.

No idea, Cyrus said, his voice the epitome of innocence.

Uh-huh, I drawled, shivering as Vox drew his fingers up the back of my thighs.

"Turn over, Claire," he said. "We'll clean you up with our mouths."

Sol grinned, clearly in favor of that idea. "Yes, turn over, little flower. I'll start with your breasts."

Enjoy, Cyrus whispered across my mind, then disappeared as Vox and Sol took control of my body,

15

moving me to my back and devouring me just like they'd promised.

By the time they were done, I couldn't even remember my name.

Which was completely okay.

Who needs a name anyway?

CYRUS

"WELL, our plan seems to be going well," I said conversationally.

"She is usually pretty agreeable after a good fucking," Titus agreed, his hand slipping into the pocket of his dress pants. He'd chosen to wear black slacks and a button-down shirt with the sleeves rolled to his elbows. No tie. It was the Fire Fae's definition of professional attire.

Mine differed from his, my wardrobe containing over a dozen suits for occasions just like this. Exos maintained a similar style. Which was why we both stood in three-piece suits.

"Is everything in place for tonight?" my half brother asked, his sapphire gaze a much-darker shade of blue than my own icy irises. But we had the same blond hair, courtesy of our Spirit Fae mother.

"Yep," Titus replied, the picture of ease with his windswept auburn locks and easygoing smile. "I have the keys to the cabin, River helped me stock the fridge with popular human food, and we moved the two king beds out of the bedrooms to push them together in the living area. Everything's a go."

I nodded. "Excellent. Now we just have to convince our little queen to accept the trials."

"Let's hope this meeting goes well," Exos replied, his expression sharpening. "We need her to be happy and agreeable."

"A few orgasms can help with that," Titus drawled.

"Not if she's unwilling to accept them," Exos tossed back. "This idea means a great deal to her. It's also important to us and our potential offspring."

"We're all aware of what's at stake," I murmured. "So let's see who we can schmooze to pave the way for our mate's success."

Titus grimaced. "I'd rather just light the opposition on fire."

"Let's call that our backup plan, hmm?" I suggested.

The Fire Fae heaved a long-suffering sigh. "Fine. I'll try the diplomatic route first. But if anyone so much as speaks out against Claire today, I'm setting them on fire."

I considered pointing out how that could lead to a battle of fae powers in the Human Realm—which would be very bad—but decided not to comment.

Titus would do whatever the fuck he wanted, with or without our consent.

Trying to convince him otherwise was a futile task.

So I just shrugged and went back to surveying the crowd.

We were meeting on neutral ground in Greenland, where the Interrealm Fae Council maintained a territory shrouded in protection. The mortals had no idea this civilization existed; it was all hidden through a variety of fae magic.

To the mortal eye, this territory resembled an uninhabitable glacier. But once a fae traversed through the enchanted boundary, a city of warmth and color was revealed.

Not all fae chose to remain in their own kingdoms—a recent development encouraged through a variety of events—and several of those fae had chosen to reside here.

I wasn't sure of the current population numbers, but it continued to rise.

We stood in the center of the city, near the main hall, where the Interrealm Fae Council chose to convene annually. Our mate wanted to start a school here for those with cross-species abilities, otherwise known as abominations.

Many fae were anti cross-species breeding because of the events of our past, but Claire was determined to fix the perception. She had several powerful allies on her side, including support from the Midnight Fae and Fortune Fae.

Claire felt that if abominations and Halflings had been more accepted as a society, her path to queendom would have been easier because she would have been welcomed and provided with the training she'd needed.

Her allies from the Midnight Fae and Fortune Fae kingdoms were also driven by personal reasons, most of which stemmed from their own trials in life.

Claire had presented her idea to their respective leadership first and had used their feedback for her presentation today. And I really could not wait to see my mate in action.

Speaking of my mate, I thought, smiling as she entered the grand hall with Sol and Vox on either side of her.

She headed right for me, her blue eyes holding a touch of the panic I felt radiating around her spirit. I immediately sent a reassuring squeeze through our bond, doing my best to calm her nerves.

"Do you have the letter?" she asked by way of greeting.

"You think I would forget it?" I countered, arching a brow.

"Cyrus."

"Claire."

She stared me down, and I stared her down right back. My little queen needed some fire, and if that meant pissing her off, so be it.

The letter she wanted was the formal request from the Elemental Fae to create the Interrealm Fae Academy. I also had a similar one from the Midnight Fae. The Fortune Fae were a bit more complicated, as they divided their territories up between Alpha leaders who ruled in equal measure with their Omegas, so Gina would only be speaking on behalf of her region and would confer with the other Omegas afterward. Although, I doubted any would challenge a revered Omega like Gina.

All the other realms would require similar agreement or would forfeit their involvement in the school.

Please don't do this, Claire whispered into my thoughts. *I need your support right now, not a fight.*

What you need is to remember who you are, I countered through our mental link. *You're a queen, Claire. Now lift your chin and show off that regal neck of yours. Maybe I'll reward you with a kiss.*

She narrowed her gaze.

I merely arched my brow back.

Was I being an ass? Yes. Was it distracting her from her nerves? Also yes.

She stepped into my personal space to start searching my jacket pockets for the letter, her hands roaming all over my torso and causing my lips to twitch with amusement. "Where is it?" she demanded, a hint of hysteria touching her gaze.

I caught her chin and held her gaze. "Breathe," I told her. *Don't let anyone see you panic, Claire. You need to walk into that meeting like you own the room. This is a brilliant idea. Fucking own it.*

Her nostrils flared. *How can I do that if you left the letter at home?*

I didn't leave it at home, little queen. I kept it safe, just like you asked, and I'll present it when you request it during the meeting. I released her jaw to cup her cheek. *Where is all this anxiety coming from, Claire? What are you afraid of?*

That they're going to hate this idea, she whispered back at me. *That... that they won't accept me or the school. Which is exactly what I don't want to happen to anyone else in my position.*

I pressed my lips to hers, hiding the tears welling in her eyes. She just needed this moment to bolster her strength, and so I provided it with my mouth while the others closed ranks around us, ensuring no one could see our queen's nervousness over this proposal.

It meant a lot to her on a personal level, making this more emotional overall. I understood that. But I needed her to understand that queens bowed to no one.

"You will go into that room and show them what a queen looks like," I told her softly. "I won't accept anything less from you, Claire."

She swallowed. "What if they hate it?"

"Then you change their minds."

Her blue eyes sparkled, the tears bleeding into something more passionate. "I don't accept a negative answer," she said slowly. "I make them say yes."

"Exactly," I replied. "They're not allowed to say no."

"They're not allowed to say no," she repeated, nodding with me. "Okay."

"Okay," I echoed back at her, pressing my lips to hers once more. "You're going to be magnificent, little queen. And we're all here if you need us."

"Thank you," she murmured, a hint of color staining her pale complexion. Not embarrassed, but excited. "I can do this."

"I know you can," I agreed. "Kick their asses. And if anyone opposes, Titus will light them on fire."

"Damn right I will," he said, nodding behind her.

Claire giggled. "That's not very diplomatic."

The Fire Fae rolled his eyes. "Fae, you sound just like Cyrus and Exos."

"I personally take that as a compliment," my brother replied, his sapphire gaze alight with approval as he studied our mate.

I released her, aware of what he wanted, and watched as he pulled her into a reassuring kiss. Titus grabbed her next, then Sol, and finally Vox, leaving our little queen winded and breathless by the end.

But she looked ready to slay.

"I'm ready," she said.

"I know," I replied. "Lead the way, little queen."

TITUS

CLAIRE RESEMBLED a goddess as she answered questions from the head of the table, her stature poised and confident, her expression jubilant.

My mate was born for leadership, just like Exos and Cyrus, who both stood beside her now.

I hung out in the back, observing everyone and monitoring Claire's mood through our bond. All this council shit wasn't for me. I preferred to handle discord with my fists, not clever words, thus making it a good thing Claire had mates like Exos, Cyrus, and Vox for balance.

"I don't like the way that Shifter Fae is acting around our mate," Sol grumbled beside me, his eyes on the vibrant-haired male talking to Claire.

"He's a peacock," Vox replied. "It's in his nature to strut like that."

"Well, if he keeps cocking his head like that, he's going to become a featherless bird," Sol muttered back at him. "Actually, isn't that what River said to cook for Thank You Day?"

"He said we need a turkey," Vox corrected. "And I think it's called Thanks Day, without the 'you.'"

"Thanks Day, then. But what's the difference between a peacock and a turkey?" Sol asked.

"I… I don't know." Vox glanced around the big guy to look at me. "What's the difference between a peacock and a turkey? They're both birds, right?"

"How the fuck would I know?" I wasn't the chef in our mate-circle. I also knew nothing about human food.

"We'll have to ask River," Vox said.

"Or we could pluck that flirty shifter and roast him instead," Sol muttered, his earthy gaze narrowing as the brightly dressed male tossed his feathered head back on a laugh.

My lips twitched. "At least he seems to be entertaining Claire's ideas." Unlike several other fae council members in the room.

The notion of an Interrealm Fae Academy stirred a great deal of conflicting results. Some were open to the idea. Others felt it would only exacerbate the abomination issue.

And then there were those who had chosen to miss the meeting entirely—namely, the Hell Fae.

I would never forget the day Cyrus and Exos explained the various kingdoms to Claire, and her horrified reaction to learning demon-like fae existed.

"You told me demons weren't real!" she'd snapped. "And werewolves, too. You… you said that was all human bullshit, or whatever."

"Technically, demons and werewolves don't exist, so I didn't really lie," Exos had replied in that holier-than-thou tone he seemed to favor.

"Yes, the appropriate terms for them are *Hell Fae* and *Shifter Fae*," Cyrus had added.

Claire had just glowered at them both, then she'd stomped outside to release a stunning array of elements that had left us all in awe of her talents. Afterward, she'd returned with a great deal of questions.

However, after learning about the Hell Fae's penchant for stealing fae for their bride trials, she hadn't been all that eager to meet them. So I supposed it was a good thing they kept skipping the meetings.

Except, she had mentioned wanting them here. Something about how they would appreciate the school since their breed of fae had been created through a series of abominations. She felt that it meant they could aid in the organization of the school programs, and had also commented on how maybe a little collaboration between the realms would help cool some of their notorious ire toward the other fae.

An optimistic outlook, one I admired her for sharing. But it would never come to fruition. The Hell Fae had no interest in reconciling with the kingdoms that had basically cast them all to the underworld—hence their name.

Sol stiffened beside me as two Paradox Fae approached Claire with glowing swords on their hips. Exos shook hands with one of them, his expression stoic and regal. Cyrus followed suit.

"I've never liked time dwellers," I muttered, agreeing with Sol's aggressive stance. "They're tricky little buggers."

Those swords on their hips were tokens that allowed them to alter timelines, leaving everyone around them none the wiser. Who knew how many realities had been shifted under their authority? Just the thought gave me chills. For a Fire Fae, not much gave me that effect.

"They'll definitely demand a price for their involvement," Vox said, his tone diplomatic. "But they love making deals."

Well, that was one outlook on their kind. An outlook far more positive than mine.

After the Paradox Fae finished, another clan of Shifter Fae approached. Each animal type had their own councilman or councilwoman, and most seemed to be represented.

On and on it went with each fae kingdom voicing their questions and concerns and only a few verbally agreeing to the idea. Others wanted more time to think, or they needed to discuss it among their own councils.

Claire positively glowed with excitement as it all came to an end, her cheeks a beautiful pink shade that reminded me of the spirit butterflies she enjoyed conjuring.

I grinned at her, eager to take her back to the cabin we'd arranged for the week. She had no idea what surprise lay in wait for her, but first, we had to eat.

Part of me wanted to skip the meal pleasantries and go straight to dessert. But Claire would need her strength later for our first trial.

Assuming she agreed to our plans.

My stomach tightened in anticipation. Part of the fun would be convincing her to indulge us in the games we had planned. And the prize would be watching her grow round with a little fae child.

Claire was already stunning, but there was just something so hot about the idea of her being pregnant with our children. She would make a beautiful mother. I couldn't wait to see it.

I just hoped she said yes.

We all did.

It'd been difficult to keep our plans from her, specifically as she was linked to all of us mentally. However, we'd somehow pulled it off. Perhaps because she'd been so wrapped up in her Interrealm Fae Academy plans.

She glanced at me, her blue eyes twinkling with so much joy my heart hurt. Then her lips curled into a secret smile as she sent fire to dance over my fingertips. I returned the gesture with a little stroke along her neck that made her visibly shiver.

You look hungry, she said into my mind.

I'm always hungry, sweetheart, I replied, the innuendo thick in my voice. *Do you want to be my appetizer?*

I think dessert is probably best.

Took the words right out of my head, I drawled, because she really had since I'd just thought something similar a few seconds ago. *I look forward to devouring you later, Claire.*

Likewise, fire mate, she murmured, blowing me a fire kiss that landed on the edge of my mouth. I drew a line of flames across her bottom lip in response, then Exos leaned in to lick it off with his tongue.

Spoilsport, I thought, rolling my eyes.

He winked back at me, then kissed her again before turning to lead the group our way.

Dinnertime.

Then… dessert.

CLAIRE

THE ICY AIR blew with a fury outside the restaurant windows, displaying the true nature of this part of Greenland. Yet, inside, we were warm and cozy and completely unimpacted by the elements.

An entire fae city was being built under this dome of magic. We were sitting on the outskirts of it all, in the pub closest to the exit. What I liked about this location was the food—they catered to all fae kind.

Which was how I'd ended up with a bowl of pasta bolognese.

It had been listed under Midnight Fae cuisine since the vampire-like beings tended to frequent the Human Realm for blood snacks. From what I understood of their culture, they'd adopted mostly human foods into their world as a result because it was all they ever ate.

Worked for me.

But I did pair it with a spritemead, because yum.

My mates all had elemental-themed dishes, while the Fortune Fae at our table had decided on some items similar to mine.

And all around us were tables filled with different types of fae.

I loved it, this feeling of togetherness among the

realms. It gave me a glimmer of hope that this Interrealm Fae Academy might actually kick off.

A spark of Winter Fae magic tickled my nose, drawing my focus out the windows once more. Fae magic still amazed me, particularly as I could sense the essence humming across my skin like a live wire.

The waves left behind a foreign kiss that called to my water magic. An icy swirl danced along my fingertips in response—one Cyrus responded to with a trickle of his own power.

My lips quirked upward in response, the sensation one that called to my very soul.

You like that, little queen? he asked, his icy blue eyes meeting mine from across the table.

I responded by increasing the flow of water around my fingertips, only to jolt as he matched my speed and took control of it with his own ties to the source. He was the Water Fae King, granting him unlimited power when it came to his element.

He sat beside his cousin Kalt, who was currently serving as a dignitary intern in one of the other fae realms.

Winter Fae, I thought, glancing outside for the fifth or sixth time tonight. They were the ones behind the magic here in Greenland because they used a similar shielding power up in the North Pole.

All those stories about Santa and his elves? Yeah, they stemmed from a real place. It had blown my mind when I first learned about it, and I was dying to visit someday. They were working closely with the Elemental Fae, mostly because they already resided in neutral territory in the Human Realm. And they were rather kind, too.

Kalt leaned in to ask Cyrus yet another question, one

my mate accepted with a contemplative nod before replying.

My heart warmed at the sight of their mentorship. I rather liked this nurturing side of my Water Fae mate. Although, it hadn't escaped my notice that he seemed far more patient with Kalt than he was with me.

"Oh, so the trials have started, then," Gina said from beside me, her voice holding a touch of excitement.

The water swirling around my fingers dissipated into mist as Cyrus focused on the Fortune Fae, his gaze narrowing. "Don't do that."

She blinked her soft blue eyes at him. "Don't do what?"

"Play in the future," he snapped.

"That's akin to telling you not to indulge your affinity for water," she retorted, frowning. "Does that mean I'm ahead? Because the path is pretty well formed."

"It is," her mate, Zeke, agreed softly, his blond hair flirting with his shoulders from the gentle breeze Vox had just conjured from the opposite end of the table. "But I think we might be in that timeline now, Dreamcatcher."

"Oh." Her full lips twisted to the side. "Right."

"What trials?" I asked, confused by her sudden commentary. Of course, I rarely understood her random statements. The woman loved to talk in riddles and often didn't make any sense at all. But we'd grown closer over the last few years. Mostly because we shared a lot of the same political motivations.

It wasn't always that way, though. I hadn't liked her at all when we'd first met. She'd been just as cryptic then, saying something about a dark piece that didn't fit. A dark piece that had turned out to be a lot closer to us than any of us had realized. Alas, that was in the past now.

However, I'd strongly disliked Gina on sight because of her stunning looks and the way Exos and Cyrus had clearly displayed a history of knowing her. Fortunately, they'd only shared a friendship.

A friendship that appeared to be in jeopardy now as they were both glowering at the Fortune Fae.

Zeke cleared his throat. "Just because I'm blind doesn't mean I can't *see*," he said. "Don't look at my mate like that."

"Okay. What's going on?" I demanded. "Why are you all so tense? What trials are coming? Is this because of the school?"

A few fae at a nearby table stopped talking, their pointy ears all angled our way, my tone having caught their attention.

I wanted to smile and wave them off, but I was too concerned about Gina's cryptic commentary to focus on diplomatic niceties.

Kalt cleared his throat. "I'm going to get another spritemead."

No one replied, everyone too busy staring between my mates and Gina.

"Um...," Aflora hummed by way of greeting, then glanced up at the tall Midnight Fae beside her— Guardian Zephyrus. "We've clearly missed something important."

Aflora had mentioned joining us a little later for dinner, saying she needed to take care of a task. She hadn't elaborated, but then, she rarely did. The Royal Earth Fae I once knew had blossomed into a powerful queen-like female with peculiar magic that many other fae feared.

But she was exactly why an Interrealm Fae Academy

needed to exist—so we could better understand abominations and the matings of power.

"Are you causing trouble?" Aflora asked, her blue-black eyebrow arching upward at Gina. The two of them had history. Something about a coffee shop. So I wasn't surprised that she immediately suspected the Fortune Fae of playing a word game. Her kind was rather notorious for it. At least she hadn't taken out her infamous card deck.

"Why does everyone assume I'm always to blame?" Gina demanded.

"Because you usually are," a Paradox Fae drawled from the bar.

"No one asked you, Kali."

"Pretty sure you just asked the entire realm," she tossed back.

Gina huffed a breath. "All I mentioned were trials," she muttered.

"Trials?" Aflora repeated, her cerulean blue eyes locking on Zephyrus.

He lifted one of his broad shoulders. "Fuck if I know." He wrapped his arm around her, then bent to whisper something in her ear. Whatever it was caused her cheeks to flush scarlet. I didn't know the Midnight Fae male well, but Cyrus and Exos enjoyed his directness. It seemed Aflora did as well, because her eyes flashed from whatever he'd said.

I stopped looking at them and stared Gina down. "Explain."

"Ask your mates," she replied. "They know what I'm talking about."

"Have you seen who wins?" Titus asked suddenly, causing Cyrus to growl at him. "Oh, come on, you're wondering the same thing I am."

"I don't want to know," Sol put in. "I want to play the game, fair and square."

"What game?" I asked. "What the hell are all of you talking about?"

"I don't need Gina to predict the winner," Cyrus replied, his focus on Titus. "We already know it's going to be me."

"Bullshit," Titus tossed back. "I beat you just the other night. She totally screamed louder for me."

I gasped. "Titus!"

Cyrus just chuckled. "Keep telling yourself that, Firefly."

"Call me that one more time, Royal Jackass."

"Firefly," he repeated, smirking.

Titus made a move to stand, but Sol clamped a paw on his shoulder to shove him back down while Vox released a long, drawn-out sigh.

Exos merely shook his head. "We want to have a baby, Claire," he said. "And we've devised a series of trials to determine who gets to do the honors."

I blinked at him. "I'm sorry… what?"

"And that's my cue to go," Gina said, pushing away from the table. "You're all welcome, by the way."

"Pretty sure none of us thanked you," Cyrus replied.

"Yeah, totally not invited to Thank You Day," Sol added.

"It's Thanks Day," Vox corrected.

"Whatever," my Earth Fae mate growled back. "She's *not* invited."

"Are you talking about Thanksgiving?" Zephyrus asked.

"Thanksgiving?" Sol repeated, his dark brows drawing down. "That doesn't even make sense as a word."

"But Thanks Day does?" Zephyrus countered.

"Seriously, I want to know who wins," Titus said, his forest-green eyes on Gina. He drew his fingers through his red hair and gave her a beautiful smile. "It's me, right."

She just grinned. "Well, it's been great. I'll see you all next month at the nesting party."

"Baby shower," Zeke said as he pushed to his feet beside her, his motions fluid and somehow regal, even while being blind.

"Yes. Right. Baby shower," she agreed.

Not that I was paying attention to them.

I was too busy gaping at the table.

Except, what had they just said? "Baby shower?" I repeated on a squeak.

"Yes, but fae call it a nesting party," she replied, already walking away with her mate, his hand on the small of her back. "Oh, and you're going to need the Hell Fae to agree. I suggest you meet with one of Lucifer's Hellhounds. But don't let Cyrus near them. If he douses their flames, they won't agree to your proposal." She gave a little wave, then started toward the exit.

"Hold on," I called after her.

But she didn't listen, instead turning the corner before I could ask what the hell she was going on about. I almost chased after her, but she had already stepped through the doors, disappearing into the snowy beyond. She'd be in a portal in the next few seconds, traveling to wherever she wanted to go.

No wonder she'd recommended eating at the restaurant by the border.

She knew this was going to happen.

Damn Fortune Fae!

34

"Someone had better start explaining things to me," I said, not in the mood for any more word games.

"I already did," Exos replied calmly. "We want to have a baby, Claire. And rather than ask you to choose who gets to be the first father, we've devised a series of trials to help determine a winner."

I gaped at him. "What if I don't want a baby?"

He didn't even bat an eye, saying, "Then we won't bother with the trials." Except I felt the pain instantly spike through my bonds, all my male mates suddenly concerned that I might turn them down.

Even Vox had a wary note to his silver-rimmed gaze.

Aflora cleared her throat again. "Uh, I think, we're just going to, uh, go…" She spoke so softly I almost didn't hear her. And as rude as it was, I couldn't even reply. I was too consumed by the emotions thriving through my bonds.

My mate-circle had spoken about children several times over the years.

Cyrus needed an heir for the Water Kingdom.

Exos also required an heir for the Spirit Kingdom.

Vox had chosen a profession in teaching because he enjoyed philosophical studies, but he also possessed a soft spot for children and watching them learn.

Sol wanted a little one of his own to nurture and grow.

And Titus, well, he tried to pretend that practicing the art of mating was all that interested him, but I caught the flickers of excitement in his thoughts around having a little fae to play Fae Ball with.

They all wanted kids.

Not necessarily one of their own—except for maybe Exos and Cyrus, who had royal duties involved—but the others just wanted to expand our circle with little fae.

Even my two king mates wanted that, despite their obligations to their thrones.

This went beyond duty for all of them.

They just wanted to create life.

Which was an Elemental Fae's greatest gift.

But I could also sense their willingness to wait, if that was what I desired. They didn't want to push me. They also didn't want to make me choose. Hence, the trials.

I couldn't discern the details from their thoughts, their minds closing off around whatever they had planned.

However, anticipation hummed through my veins, ready for whatever they had in store.

"Okay," I said slowly, looking at each of my mates. "Tell me about these trials."

CLAIRE

"OKAY, I'm going to need you to go back to the orgasm trial again." There'd been other items mentioned, but that was the competition that had captured my interest.

Titus smirked. "It's exactly what it sounds like, and we intended to start here tonight." He gestured around the cabin my mates had sequestered me off to in Iceland, of all places.

After we'd paid for the food and drink bill at the Fae Pub—yes, that was the extremely original name—and Cyrus had said goodbye to his cousin, my mates had portalled me to the middle of the woods where a cabin waited with a very large bed inside.

I suspected they'd taken the beds from the guest rooms and just pushed them together in the center of the living area, because the sheets were a bit haphazard, and the size of the mattress definitely wasn't common in the human world.

Regardless, it worked.

And I really wanted to start the orgasm trial... like, now.

"So you're all just... going to see how many orgasms you can force out of me over the next five days." I did not see a problem with this logic. At all.

"Six days," Titus corrected. "We decided the first one doesn't count because of the excitement. So we'll warm you up properly for a day, then we each get a twenty-four-hour period."

I swallowed. "Oh, okay," I said. "Um. Yeah, we can start now."

Exos grinned. "So eager."

"We need you to agree to all the trials first, little queen," Cyrus murmured. "And we also need to know you're really okay with the outcome. Are you ready to have a baby with us?"

All five of them studied my reaction, my mates always putting my comfort above their own. Was I ready to have a baby? I wasn't sure. Was anyone ever ready?

But I knew in my heart that my mates would be amazing fathers.

They would help me through this, protect me, and love me unconditionally. All facts I felt through our bond yet already knew.

Because they'd been there for me from the beginning, even before we were fully mated.

The six of us were made for this, and if my mates wanted a baby, then so did I. We were in this together, forever and always.

Besides, I rather liked the idea of making them all fathers.

They'd all make some sexy fae dads.

But that wasn't the reason I really wanted to do this.

My reason was simply because it felt like it was time. I hadn't really noticed it before, but I could sense it now. Our mate-circle was ready to create a new life.

"I'm scared," I admitted. "Because I don't really know what to expect. But I trust you guys. And if you all are ready, then so am I."

"Don't do this for us, Claire," Exos replied, stepping up to cup my cheek with his palm. "This needs to be because you really want it, too."

"I do want it," I whispered, leaning into his touch. "It… it feels right. Fae create life. I want to create a life with all of you."

I knew only one of them could actually plant the seed, but it would be a shared experience nonetheless. Because we were a unit.

I opened my heart and mind to all of them, allowing them to feel my acceptance and love, and melted beneath their responding waves of adoration and devotion.

Then Exos captured my mouth in a mind-blowing kiss that ignited the first trial. This was meant to ease me into the experience, to sate my mind and body and prepare me for the pleasures and pains to come.

Having a child wouldn't be easy.

We all knew that.

This was about worship, to prove to me that my mates would see to my every need, to be there for me through it all.

They wanted me pliable and agreeable, too.

But most importantly, they wanted me to feel how much they loved me.

I returned their ardor with my spirit, embracing each of them with the heart of my being while falling headfirst into Exos's kiss.

It was hot, fiery passion, burning into an inferno as Titus stepped up to my back to grab my hips. Exos's lips went to my neck, his hands unzipping my jacket, which Titus then removed from my shoulders and dragged down my arms.

Cyrus took it from him, tossing it to the side. Then

he switched spots with Exos, his mouth claiming mine as his palms slid up beneath my sweater. I shivered against his cool touch, my skin fire to his ice. Then Titus's hands met my bare back, his thumb drawing fire down my spine.

I groaned, the onslaught of elemental powers alighting me from the inside out and calling my own affinities to life.

My sweater incinerated to ash, Titus's essence roaming possessively over me as he drew his blazing touch down my jeans.

He sliced through the fabric with a fiery blade, destroying my pants and scattering the remains in a dust of embers on the ground.

Cyrus smiled against my mouth. "That is so handy, Firefly."

Titus growled in response, his hand leaving my back and reaching up for a fistful of Cyrus's blond hair. "One more time, Jackass. One. More. Time."

"Firefly," Cyrus taunted, grinning at whatever expression Titus gave him over my shoulder.

Their aggression had my thighs clenching at the underlying sexual tension. They sometimes played with each other, but only when I joined. Unlike Sol and Vox, who sometimes shared a bed. I didn't mind, because I felt their connection to me the whole time, and I often crept in to join them after a heavy-petting session.

Our bonds were special because we all loved each other, too.

Even when Cyrus and Titus pretended to be at odds with one another.

I wrapped my arms around Cyrus's waist as Titus pushed me closer to him, fully sandwiching me between them. Then he yanked Cyrus's mouth to his own, the two of them engaging in a feral and harsh kiss.

The lace of my panties soaked right through, their virile display almost enough to make me orgasm on the spot.

That I could feel their hard bodies on either side of me only intensified the moment.

Then a palm on the back of my nape yanked me toward another hungry mouth. *Sol.* My rock. My Earth Fae mate. I melted into him while Cyrus and Titus continued to duel on either side of me.

It was gratifyingly intense and beautiful and grounded me in the reality of my circle.

So much passion and heat.

One of them palmed my breast. *Titus.*

The other cupped my sex. *Cyrus.*

And still they dueled with their tongues as Sol devoured me with his own.

I moaned, on fire from the sensations and eager to feel more.

Cyrus slid my panties aside, making me wonder why I ever bothered with the undergarment as he dipped two fingers into me and speared upward. I cried out, then whimpered for more.

He rewarded me with another thrust, his thumb sliding upward to flick my clit. An orgasm flared out of me as though he'd demanded it to rise, causing my knees to buckle and my body to alight with renewed flames.

Titus caught me with his arm around my waist, his pronounced erection digging into my backside. My forehead went to Cyrus's shoulder, Sol's palm still around my nape, as my males held me through the aftershocks of the too-sudden pleasure.

"This is why we needed a warm-up day," Titus said.

"Yes," Cyrus agreed. "Too easy."

I really wanted to remark on that, but I didn't have enough air in my lungs to speak. Nor was my brain functioning well enough to muster up a comeback. So I settled on a grunting sound instead that had all my mates chuckling around me.

"Finishing stripping her," Cyrus demanded.

Titus's fiery energy warmed my breasts, the lace disintegrating in a second. Then the same sensation traveled to my shaved mound and lower, causing me to jolt upright on a moan. "She's ready again," he mused, his power stroking through my slickened lips before he used his gift to incinerate my panties.

Sol went to his knees beside me to handle my boots and socks, removing them with hands gentle and sure. Then he stroked his fingers up my calf to my thigh before wrapping his palm around the back of my leg and tugging me toward his waiting mouth.

A curse slipped from my lips as his tongue met my clit, my legs giving out again. But Titus caught me with ease as Cyrus stepped out of the way for Vox to join the fun. I gazed up at him through hooded eyes, my body convulsing and limp from Sol's ministrations below.

I expected my Air Fae mate to kiss me, but instead he dipped his head to my breasts, sucking a nipple deep into his mouth before gently grazing the tip with his teeth.

I threaded my fingers through his long, dark hair, holding him to me as he taunted me with his skilled tongue.

Sol seemed to replicate the pace between my legs, his rhythm rivaling Vox's in every way.

Then Titus reached between my legs from behind to draw some of my wetness backward to my other hole. I groaned as he slid a finger inside, working to stretch me and prepare me for the night to come.

They would use me just as I would use them.

And together, we would fall into a heated mess of limbs and naked bodies.

Yet I was the only one without clothes right now, all my mates still fully dressed.

That wouldn't do.

I took a page from Titus's playbook and destroyed their outfits with a flick of my mind. Or I tried to, anyway. It worked on Vox and Sol, their clothes disappearing beneath a wave of my power. Their shoes were somewhere by the door, so I left those alone.

But my other mates had anticipated my play. Exos and Titus had created a wall of their own fire guarding their fabric, and Cyrus had countered me with water.

My eyes fluttered open to find the two kings smirking at me, daring me to try harder.

It served as an aphrodisiac, heightening the moment and cascading me beneath an avalanche of challenge and intrigue. Sol and Vox kept their mouths on me, my fingers weaving through their soft hair, holding them exactly where I needed, while Titus held me in place for their feasting mouths. He increased his pressure on my backside, causing me to cry out in agony-induced pleasure, my body on literal fire for them all.

I wanted to be filled by them, to be taken to heaven and back by my mates, and to land in a pile of sweaty limbs.

But I knew this was just the beginning.

They never rushed, their mouths and touch thorough to the very end.

Sol sucked my clit deep into his mouth while Vox skimmed my nipple with his teeth. Then Titus added another finger below, stretching me deliciously and warming me up for an evening of sex.

Yet three of my mates remained clothed, and I needed to fix that. But, oh, I wasn't sure how. Not with Sol's tongue moving like that. And Vox, *Fae*, his lips... *mmm...*

Titus chuckled against my ear. "Focus, sweetheart." He scissored his fingers. "You'll need to disrobe all of us if you want us to fuck you."

"Or Sol and Vox can do it for you," I replied on a moan, my body undulating wantonly between them all.

"You'd prefer I fuck Titus?" Cyrus taunted, sending a wave of heat through my veins as the mental image appeared in my mind.

They were always bickering, the sexual tension between them off the charts. And the idea of Cyrus bending Titus over and driving into him? Yeah, that had my thighs clenching around Sol in severe anticipation.

"I hope you brought lube, Firefly," Cyrus murmured, his icy gaze full of wicked intent.

"Not happening, Royal Jackass," Titus returned, his teeth skimming my throat. "But you're welcome to suck my cock."

"I only kneel for Claire," Cyrus replied, his expression heating. "However, I would consider a temporary position, if that's her desire."

I groaned at the thought, my climax mounting as Sol pushed me over the edge with his tongue. And then I was too busy kissing Vox to understand up from down.

My mates were consuming me, just like they always did. Throwing out hot suggestions one moment and distracting me the next.

I tried to focus on one task, only to be thrown headfirst into another as Titus carried me to the bed.

"Spread your legs for Sol," he demanded. "We'll see if his cock is enough to satisfy you."

Clothes, I thought. *I have to remove their clothes.*

That was the game… tonight's challenge… to see if I could focus long enough to disrobe them.

And when I won, they'd reward me with their bodies.

Sol climbed over me, his muscles rippling as he bent to suck my nipple into his mouth before sliding in between my thighs. "So wet," he mused, nibbling a path up to my jaw. "Wrap your stems around me, little flower."

My thighs cradled him as I hooked my ankles against his ass, urging him forward. He took it for the invitation it was, filling me to the hilt and stretching me deliciously around him. I arched, my sensitive insides protesting the invasion while also squeezing him in warm welcome, begging for more.

It was such a conundrum.

My mates had taught me how to receive hours of pleasure, all of them able to take me over and over again without growing tired.

It was a whole new definition of stamina that made me all the more thankful for my fae half.

Sol captured my mouth in a searing kiss, his body bathing me in an earth scent underlined in heat and sex. Vitality blossomed inside me, embracing my spirit and grounding me thoroughly in the moment of his clear claim.

Only, fire danced along my arms, followed by a trickle of water that reminded me I had other mates waiting.

They were teasing me.

Watching Sol fuck me.

Engaging my elements and forcing me to play their

game.

I groaned, a cataclysm of eroticism ripping through my soul and calling my elements to the surface.

Air.

Water.

Earth.

Fire.

Spirit.

All of them danced through the room, crawling along the walls in real vines decorated with pink butterflies and fiery embers. Water swirled with the flames, dancing to the same pace as Sol's hips, and heat erupted in my lower belly as another orgasm shredded my ability to breathe.

Vox was suddenly there, his mouth on mine, blowing air into my lungs, rejuvenating me with his essence as he lay alongside me. His arousal touched my hip, then Sol reached down to fist him. My Air Fae mate jolted, a growl vibrating his tongue against mine.

Goose bumps pebbled along my arms and legs, the lust of the two men overwhelming me in the best way.

I allowed them to take their pleasure, reveling in their need and letting it suffocate me beneath a cloud of ecstasy.

Sol sank his teeth into my shoulder as he came inside me, his seed hot and filling me with his earthy essence, while Vox shot off beside me, his cum a welcome substance against my skin.

But Titus had been right.

It wasn't enough.

I needed more.

My mates who still wore clothes.

And I suddenly knew just what I needed to do to convince them to strip.

EXOS

CLEVER LITTLE MATE, I thought, watching the minx roll around in the sheets, painting herself with Sol's and Vox's cum.

She'd started with a finger through her slick pussy, drawing Sol's essence up her shaved mound to rub into her skin. Then she'd taken the remnants of Vox's pleasure along her ribs and painted the rosy little peaks of her breasts.

I never would have thought my mate drenched in the cum of other men would turn me on, but here we were. And all I wanted to do was strip myself and add to the mess.

The tension radiating from my brother said he felt the same.

My tie was suddenly a little too tight. I loosened it while Claire watched, and her blue eyes flashed. "I know what you're doing, baby," I told her.

"Do you?" she asked, her tone falsely innocent as she dipped her hand between her legs again to slip her fingers through her pretty pink lips. Sol and Vox lounged on either side of her, content for the moment, while the rest of her mates stood around the bed with raging hard-ons, fully clothed.

She brought her finger to her lips this time, groaning at the taste of her arousal mingling with Sol's seed.

It left me wondering why we'd decided to play this game. All I wanted was to sink balls-deep into my female and force my name from that alluring mouth.

I pulled off my tie, and Cyrus mimicked the motion, then took the silk from my hands. I immediately understood his intention as he approached the bed. "Give me your hands, little queen."

She smiled. "Only if you give me your shirt."

He considered her for a moment, then dropped the ties onto the bed. "All right." He shrugged out of his jacket and tossed it at Titus. The Fire Fae caught it and proceeded to destroy it with one of his hotter flames.

Cyrus smirked. "You're going to pay for that later, Firefly."

"I hate that nickname."

"Oh, I know," he returned as he unbuttoned his shirt. "It's why I'll forever call you by it."

"Royal Jackass," the Fire Fae muttered, the label one he seemed to use interchangeably between me and Cyrus. My brother adored it. I just rolled my eyes.

"Here you go, little queen," Cyrus said, dropping his shirt on the bed for her. "Now give me your hands."

Vox rolled over her to lie beside Sol, his gaze knowing as Cyrus took hold of Claire's wrists and bound them with our ties. She'd known his intention as well, but the glimmer in her eye told me that had been her plan all along.

And as his pants went up in flames half a second later, I understood why. She'd used his brief touch as a way to overpower his water magic and destroy his clothes.

My lips curled, impressed.

Cyrus rewarded her with a kiss, his own amusement at her antics clear in the way he cradled her face while devouring her mouth.

Titus watched the scene with interest, then pulled his shirt over his head and tossed it to the ground. "Fuck delayed gratification."

Something told me this had been Claire's plan as well. She knew just how to manipulate each of us with her body and mind. I slid my hands into my pockets as Titus kicked off his pants and joined the others on the bed. He went straight for her cunt, his mouth and tongue lapping up her soaked sex and causing her to moan into Cyrus's mouth.

She threaded her fingers through the Fire Fae's auburn locks, her wrists still glued together from the silk ties. Cyrus caught her hands and gently pulled them over her head. Sol clamped his palm over hers, holding them down against the pillows while Cyrus drew his fingers down her arms.

It was all so harmonious after years of playing with our mate. While we often took turns, frequently desiring nights alone with her as well, we still enjoyed moments like this. It just didn't happen as much as we would like.

Vox, Titus, and Sol resided with Claire at Elemental Fae Academy. Cyrus misted back and forth between the Academy and the Water Kingdom, sometimes taking Claire with him for brief visits. And I maintained my residence in the Spirit Kingdom but ventured back to the Academy for our group nights.

It worked for us.

Claire always spent one night a week alone with me in the Spirit Kingdom, just as she went to Cyrus for a night as well. Then Titus, Vox, and Sol all had their own evening with her at the Academy. And then we would have two full days as a mate-circle.

Which typically ended in a similar activity to the one unfolding on the bed.

"Straddle Titus," Cyrus demanded as the Fire Fae lay on his back beside Sol. Vox had propped himself up onto his elbow to watch, while the Earth Fae lounged lazily on the pillows, his protective gaze on Claire. He always ensured her safety, just as I guarded the entire circle. It was why I still stood fully clothed, watching the events play out.

I'd join last.

I almost always did.

My groin tightened as Claire lithely rolled onto Titus's hips, her body reminiscent of a goddess. Which was an apt description, given her control over all five elements.

She was a true queen.

A beauty.

A wonder in the world of fae.

And she was mine.

I licked my lips, loving the way her breasts swayed as she rocked her hips to guide Titus inside her. The Fire Fae hissed out a breath, his hands clamping down on her slender waist to hold her in place. Cyrus removed her silk binds, then threaded his fingers in her voluminous hair and guided her down to Titus's waiting mouth.

The two of them engaged in a kiss defined by their affinity for fire. I felt it heating the air, engaging my secondary ability for the element. Cyrus battled it with his water, dousing each of the embers before they could reach his fair skin. Then he moved behind Claire to line himself up with her ass.

Titus had already prepared her, something we all knew he'd done for Cyrus.

The two of them had bonded in an unexpected way over the years, their penchant for double-penetrating Claire well known and respected in our circle. Sometimes I joined them and took her mouth, but not tonight.

I wanted her last.

To make love to her.

To soothe her.

To adore her.

She'd done so well today at the Interrealm Fae Council meeting. My chest warmed with the memory, my pride radiating through the bond as she accepted Cyrus's thrust. Her pleasure shot through our link, her back arching at the impact of both men inside her. Titus palmed her tits while my brother wrapped his arm around her middle, holding her to him as he pushed deep into her backside.

Then he grabbed her hair and angled her head back for a kiss, providing the most erotically beautiful image for us all to observe.

Our mate being fucked at both ends.

Her tits cupped by a Fire Fae.

Her tongue claimed by a Water Fae King.

Sol and Vox were already aroused again, the sight of their mate's pleasure an aphrodisiac none of us could ignore. The fact that Cyrus and Titus knew how to turn her into a work of art only added to the experience.

They didn't hold back, taking her with an abandon that made her scream against Cyrus's mouth.

I unbuttoned the top of my too-tight pants, my stomach clenching with a need I barely contained. I needed her more than I needed to breathe. But I held myself back, valuing my control, guarding her while she lost herself to utter bliss between the two mates fucking her.

She created such a stunning sight, her body made for sex, made for this, made for *us*.

I sent a trail of fire down her abdomen to her clit, sending her over the edge with Titus right behind her. And then Cyrus growled, his body emptying inside her, the three of them riding out an orgasmic experience that all of us felt through our connections.

It was so intensely intimate that I almost came myself. Sol started lazily stroking himself in response. Vox just stared at the others, his silver-rimmed black gaze filled with rapturous intent.

But it was my turn to play.

Claire glanced at me with lust-blown pupils, her cheeks blushing with a mixture of exertion and excitement. Her power flared, her fire trying to destroy my clothes once more. But I shielded myself from her, desiring a proper fight that only my mate could provide.

She didn't disappoint, taking me to the spirit plane, where our souls thrived, and engaging me in a seductive twist of enchanting warmth.

I smiled, intrigued, and pulled her toward the source, longing to test her abilities and overall control. She yanked back. Then I jumped away and she followed, frolicking inside our special place while our bodies remained in the Human Realm with everyone else.

Cyrus lurked nearby, his spirit energy drawn into the playground on impulse alone. We were both sons of a Spirit Fae Royal, and most Spirit Fae had access to more than one element. His secondary element was water because of his royal father. My secondary gift was fire, which was how I battled Claire in the physical plane. But my soul belonged to the spirit element, where I often made her bow.

Except she seemed hell-bent on bringing me to my knees tonight, her flirtatious movements brushing along my side, alighting a trail of yearning in her wake.

You're getting good at this, princess, I whispered into her mind. *Even royally fucked and exhausted, you're still putting up a decent challenge.*

I learned from the best, she breathed back at me, her energy signature humming along mine once more.

She was beautiful here in her ethereal state, her essence holding a touch of pink tonight. Her happiness warmed my heart. But it was the red spot at her center that I desired—her passion and need.

I took a step toward the bed, aware of our surroundings in the cabin. Her eyes had fallen closed, her other mates giving us a little bit of space for this spiritual embrace. Cyrus lay to her left, his head on her pillow. Titus was on the right. Sol and Vox rested on Cyrus's other side.

A beautiful sight, welcoming me into the fold.

But I remained in the spiritual realm as well, chasing her all over the field near the source of my power. Most fae couldn't play this close to the anchor of our element. However, I wasn't most fae. Elemental Fae Kings were the conduit of our respective sources, and I maintained the spirit entity. As my mate, Claire could access it as well, which she proved now by darting even closer to the blinding light.

I anticipated her next move, though, and stepped into her path to catch her. She giggled, then melted into my essence, providing me with the most intimate kiss our kind could ever experience.

We weren't physically touching but mentally embracing.

And it nearly sent me to my knees.

Please, Exos, she pleaded into my mind. *I want you.*

You always want me.

I do, she agreed, ignoring my arrogance. *But tonight, I need you.* She leaned into me, her spirit weaving through mine and creating an intimate braid I would never be able to detach myself from. Not because I lacked the power to do so—I could easily dismantle it—but because I refused to ever unknot our souls. We were made for each other, and I proved it now by allowing her power to rush over me, to dissolve my clothes in the present.

You know I love you when I let you destroy one of my favorite suits, I whispered into her mind as I knelt onto the bed between her splayed legs. *Are you ready for me, baby?*

Yes, she replied, reaching blindly for me. *Fuck me, Exos.*

I bent to press a kiss to her mound. *Maybe I want to eat you instead.*

I need you inside me.

Do you? I asked, sliding a finger into her slick heat. *Like this?*

More.

I added another finger. *Better?*

Exos.

Claire.

She growled, and it was the most adorable sound. I nipped her clit in response, then licked a path up to her generous tits. She groaned beneath my touch, her fingers weaving through my hair as she yanked me fully out of the spirit realm and to the cabin around us. I could usually play in both realities, but I felt her need for my complete physical touch.

Our souls were already bound.

Now she wanted to unite our bodies.

I prowled over her, then took her mouth in a kiss meant to bruise. She accepted my cruelty, my love, my need for control, and unleashed her unspoken demands by wrapping her legs around me.

"Give her what she wants," Cyrus encouraged.

"Yeah, or I'll do it for you," Sol added in a low tone.

I chuckled and drew my dick along her damp pussy, loving the wet, welcoming kiss of her heat. "You all had your turn. She's mine now."

"Ours," Titus corrected.

"Not for this moment," I replied, sliding my cock deep into her, claiming her fully and taking her the way I preferred.

She allowed it, knowing my preferences in bed and embracing them. As did the others, even though I could practically feel Titus challenging me through the bonds. It only strengthened the moment, giving me a purpose to drive toward, a point to prove by taking our mate to new heights as I drove into her with the abandon we both needed.

Endless gratification required new twists to keep the pleasure fresh, which was what I gave her now.

A hint of pain.

A hint of violence.

A hint of male aggression.

And a whole hell of a lot of adoration.

Her tongue dueled with mine, her nails scraping down my back as I spurred her onward. Then I tightened my hold around her spirit, adding another knot to the mess she'd created and groaning as she jolted in reply.

It was a spiritual mating underlined in physical touch and heat.

She burned me from the inside out, and I returned the favor in kind.

Exos, she panted into my mind.

Now, princess, I replied, knowing what she needed. *Come for me now.*

Her back bowed off the bed, her lips parting on a scream that I swallowed with my tongue. She vibrated, her pleasure nearing pain, and her walls strangled the fuck out of my shaft. It felt amazing. Addictive. Delirious.

I pumped into her, needing more, driving her to yet another orgasm in minutes, and giving her a prelude for the competition to come.

Because I wanted to win.

Just like all the other mates.

And I had no problem pleasing my Claire.

For hours. Days. Weeks. Whatever it took.

She fell apart beneath me, her teeth digging into my lower lip in a silent reprimand for forcing so much out of her. And damn if that wasn't the sexiest response she'd ever given me.

I speared my tongue into her mouth in time with my cock below and reveled in the burn building inside my lower abdomen. Fuck, it was good. So, so *good.* Claire dug her heels into my ass, urging me onward, giving me that subtle demand she knew I loved, and encouraging me to join her in oblivion.

My balls tightened.

My stomach clenched.

The moment slowed, everything intensifying and then exploding into a million pieces as I lost myself inside her.

She was so tight. So hot. So wet. So fucking perfect.

I groaned, her name a benediction on my tongue as I

gave her everything, drenching her with my claim and kissing the life out of her along the way.

I love you, I told her. *Fuck, I love you, Claire.*

I love you, too, she breathed, her eyes fluttering closed, her exhaustion evident.

I couldn't wait to see her in a week. She'd be a replete mess of over-gratification.

"Hmm, let the orgasm trials begin," I mused, nibbling her chin.

"'kay" was all she said back, her lips pulling into a lazy grin as she fell into a sweet slumber.

"Get some sleep, little queen," Cyrus said, kissing her temple. "You're going to need it."

CLAIRE

I NEVER WANTED to come again.

Ever.

Well, for at least a few days. Maybe a week. Because yeah. I couldn't feel my lady parts. My nipples were pretty much solid glass. And yeah, I couldn't walk.

"You know, I think this whole trial thing backfired," I said conversationally. "You broke my vagina. So. I won't be having a baby after all. But thanks for all the, uh, orgasms."

Cyrus chuckled, his palm a brand against my thigh. "Trust me, you're not broken." He leaned in to kiss the pulse point of my neck. "And I bet we could all make you come again in a few hours."

I crossed my legs. "No."

Titus joined Cyrus in his amusement. The two of them had tied in the trial. Apparently, it wasn't just about the number of orgasms but also about the intensity of them and how loud I screamed.

They were all even in my book, but Cyrus and Titus claimed victory for making my aftershocks last the longest.

I hadn't been paying attention at all—too lost to blissful oblivion—so I just took their word for it.

Exos handed me a cup of his famous hot chocolate and bent to kiss me on the head. *You're majestic,* he whispered in my mind. *And you're not broken, just well fucked.*

His words drew a line of fire through my veins that caused my lower belly to pulse with want. I squirmed, the intensity too much too soon. He chuckled in response, as did Cyrus, who had felt my thigh clench beneath his hand.

Vox entered with a tray of food, his hair loose around his shoulders and his upper body shirtless. Sol followed him inside with another tray, his body similarly clad to the Air Fae. They set both platters at the foot of the bed.

"There's more in the kitchen," Vox said, winking at me.

My nose twitched at the familiar scent of bacon. "Did you…?"

"I did," he replied, reading the thought from my mind. Perhaps not literally. All my mates had to know what I was thinking.

"So this is real bacon? Like, from a pig?"

"Yep," he confirmed. "Not a troll in sight."

I set my hot chocolate on an end table and jumped up in excitement. Then I threw my arms around him just as someone cleared their throat from the doorway.

Kalt stood on the threshold wearing a winter hat, scarf, jacket, and jeans. His eyes were fixated on Cyrus, not on me, but that didn't stop Sol from grabbing my naked body and pushing me behind him. "Out," he snapped.

"Cyrus told me—"

"Out!" Sol repeated, louder this time.

I peeked around him in time to see Kalt mist somewhere else, causing me to roll my eyes.

59

"Really?" I asked my Earth Fae mate. "You could have just handed me a robe."

Which was precisely what Exos did, his manner much calmer. I slipped the silk over my arms and cinched the tie around my waist.

"We are not inviting a sixth mate into our circle," Sol grumbled.

Cyrus huffed a laugh. "Kalt has his hands full with a selkie at the moment. I think he's fine."

"A selkie?" I repeated.

"Yeah, a seal shifter," he replied. "They're a type of Winter Fae."

"Is it safe yet?" Kalt called from the other side of the door. "Or would you like to continue discussing my love life?"

"Cheeky," Cyrus murmured, grinning from ear to ear.

"I have no idea who he reminds me of," Exos deadpanned. "No idea at all."

Titus snorted and plucked a piece of bacon from the plate.

"You can come in," I called, stepping around my rock of a mate. He placed a possessive palm against my lower back, making my lips twitch. *I don't need or want more mates, Sol.*

Good. His mental voice reminded me of smooth rocks. *Because I'm not sharing you with another royal.*

You like Exos and Cyrus.

I tolerate them, he muttered.

You more than tolerate them, I replied. There'd been a time when Sol didn't trust any of them, his experience with a powerful fae having altered his opinion of Spirit Fae and royals. But he'd slowly overcome his past, even if he was trying to feign otherwise now.

I could feel his deep-seated respect for Exos and Cyrus. This was more about Kalt seeing me naked after a week of orgasms than it was about the possibility of me taking another mate. Sol didn't like anything that could potentially cause me discomfort. And for that—and a myriad of other reasons—I loved him dearly.

I'm okay, I assured him as Kalt entered again, the Water Fae's gaze wary.

"What brings you to Iceland?" I asked, genuinely curious.

"Uh, I have an update from the Winter Fae. Cyrus said you were still here, and he suggested I drop by to give you the news." He swallowed, his long white hair billowing in the wind stirred by Vox's air magic. It seemed to just flow naturally around my mate, who stood closest to the door.

"Tell her," Cyrus said, his lips curling.

Those two words told me my water mate already knew whatever Kalt intended to say.

"The Winter Fae have agreed to support the academy and enchant it like they did the Interrealm Region," Kalt announced.

"They have?" I jumped up once on a squeal, then ran across the room to hug the Water Fae emissary. He didn't return the gesture because of Sol's growl at my back.

That robe is thin and leaving nothing to the imagination, little flower.

Fae run around naked all the time, I reminded him, rolling my eyes. *Especially Earth Fae.* But I released the frozen Water Fae anyway and took a few steps back. "Sorry, I'm excited."

"I know," he replied, glancing at Cyrus. "How do you know about Norden?"

"I know a lot of things," my mate drawled. "I know about Lark, too."

Kalt made a noise. "It's not true. I'm not in their triad."

Cyrus lifted a shoulder. "Hey, I'm not one to judge."

"I'm a Water Fae, not a Winter Fae." Kalt uttered the words through his teeth, his pretty eyes blazing with icy power.

"What's a triad?" I asked, glancing between them.

"Similar to a mating circle," Exos replied. "The Winter Fae culture is a little different from ours. They form male packs that take a single female mate."

"So they're like Fortune Fae?" I guessed, thinking of Gina and her mate-circle.

Exos considered that for a moment before saying, "Hmm. Sort of. It's a comparable concept in how the males bond with each other just as much as they do with the female. However, the Winter Fae don't have the same Alpha, Beta, Omega structure."

Kalt snorted. "Tell that to Lark. The royal elf sure as fuck thinks he's an Alpha."

"That's because you keep fighting fate," Cyrus replied.

"*I am not a Winter Fae,*" he retorted, his white hair frosting at the ends. "And why are we even talking about this? I just came to deliver the declaration."

"From Lark," Cyrus added.

"Yes. From Prince Lark," he admitted, his jaw clenched. "They've agreed to support the academy and the necessary magic. Now I'm taking a few days off while the Winter Fae go play and spread Christmas cheer throughout the Human Realm."

"You should come back with us to Elemental Fae

Academy," Cyrus suggested. "You can help us with the trials."

"Trials?" he repeated, his expression morphing from confusion to exasperation. "Ah, fuck, what did Lance do now?"

I almost laughed. Lance was Titus's little brother and Kalt's best friend. And yeah, the little firecracker was a troublemaker. But he'd mostly cooperated with his probationary sentence, where he served as my assistant at the Academy. I rather liked the hotheaded fae. He reminded me of his brother, just younger and a little more wild.

"He's talking about their competition," I clarified. "For who gets to be the father of our first baby. Nothing to do with Lance."

Kalt blinked at me. Then he looked at his cousin and arched a white brow. "Why the hell would I help with that?"

"We need judges," Cyrus explained. "And last I recall, you still owed me a favor."

The Water Fae narrowed his gaze. "So this is the favor you require? Judging sex games on my days off?"

"Uh…" I cleared my throat. "I don't… I, uh…" I couldn't remember what the other trials were, as my mind had concentrated solely on the orgasm competition. "I agree with Kalt on this one." Because those trials were probably sex related.

Exos chuckled. "The other trials are all about nurturing, nonsexual endurance, and meal preparation. We need the judge specifically for the last part."

"Meal preparation?" Kalt arched his brow again. "So you need someone to judge food?"

"Essentially, yes." Exos lifted a shoulder. "All three trials blend together but end with cooking dinner. We'll

63

be relying on others to tell us who prepares the best meal."

"Free food," Kalt said. "Okay, sure. I can handle that."

Cyrus smirked. "Not enjoying the Winter Fae cuisine?"

"It's a little sweet for my liking," he admitted. "They eat cupcakes for breakfast."

"I see nothing wrong with this," I replied as I retrieved my untouched hot chocolate from the end table. "Let's go to the North Pole."

"But I made bacon." Vox waved at the plates. "And real eggs."

My lips twisted. "True. Okay, breakfast, then cupcakes."

All my mates chuckled, while Kalt remained unmoved. He clearly didn't like the idea of going back to the North Pole.

"We have to start the trials today, little queen," Cyrus said. "But once we're done, we can take you wherever you want to go."

"Why today?" I asked before taking a sip of the decadent liquid. It was so, so, so good. *I seriously love you,* I told Exos.

I love you, too, baby.

"Because we all agreed that it was best to test our endurance and nurturing after a week of pleasuring you. It increases the stakes and makes it more realistic," Cyrus explained.

"Yes, because we need to make sure we can balance fucking you and raising a child," Titus added, his trademark bluntness coming out to play. "So the next phase is to nurture a breakable object, stay awake for thirty hours, and then cook a nutritious meal."

Cyrus nodded. "We'll be evaluated on all three tests and have that added to our scores from this week."

"What kind of breakable objects?" I wondered out loud, picking up a piece of bacon to nibble on between my sips of hot chocolate. Weird, yes. But it tasted amazing.

"It's yet to be assigned," Titus replied. "And we're supposed to have an observer for that part, too."

"True." Cyrus looked at Kalt. "So you'll be judging that as well."

"He can't be your observer," Exos interjected. "He's too biased."

"You're right. He'll say I failed," Cyrus replied. "He can observe Titus."

Kalt grunted. "You realize I know nothing about caring for an object?"

"All you need to do is take notes and say how the object was treated," Vox murmured. "If Titus lights it on fire, add the observation to the notes."

Titus scoffed at that. "I'm not going to light it on fire."

"We'll see, won't we?" Vox replied, his lips curling.

My fire mate just rolled his eyes before saying, "Lance can be another judge."

"River, too," Exos suggested. "He's at the Academy, so it makes sense."

"We can also get Ophelia and Mortus to help," Cyrus said. "That gives us five observers for the nurturing trial. They can also confirm we didn't fall asleep for thirty hours. And afterward, everyone will join us for dinner."

"It's settled, then," Exos agreed, clasping his hands together. "So let's eat, then we'll head back and find our items."

I smiled around my mug of hot chocolate.

This was going to be amusing as hell.

Good luck, boys, I thought at them all, then lost myself to breakfast.

Because bacon was almost as good as sex.

TITUS

"WHAT IS THAT?" I asked, eyeing the translucent sphere in Cyrus's hand. It resembled a glass orb with ice crystals etched along the outside.

"It's an ice relic from the Winter Fae realm," Cyrus replied, using his water magic to keep it frozen. "I asked Kalt to bring me one."

"It's beautiful," Claire said, her element stroking the item tenderly. "What did you find, Titus?"

I cleared my throat, suddenly nervous. Why did Cyrus have to go show me up with a relic from another realm? Dick. Not all of us had access to foreign objects. At least mine was elemental related. I gently unrolled my pouch to present my fragile item for Claire.

"It's a Firebird egg," I said. "An infertile one, so it's technically edible." I hadn't wanted to risk a life in this trial. Perhaps that was counterproductive to the nurturing part of the test, but Firebirds were beautiful and rare and very protective of their unborn young.

"I love Firebirds." Claire's eyes took on a dreamy quality, her mind picturing one of the stunning fiery creatures. They reminded me of phoenixes, only smaller.

Vox, Sol, and Exos all went next, displaying their items for Claire in a similar fashion.

Vox had a feather.

Sol had a peach from Claire's favorite tree at the Academy.

And Exos held an enchanted hand mirror, one that could function as a portal key to peek into other realms. He demonstrated by showing her a picture of her home in Ohio, which earned him the biggest grin of all.

"Oh, I miss it there." Our mate sounded so wistful, which only further confirmed that our plans for her were the right ones. "The pumpkin patch and corn mazes were always so fun." We watched a kid run through one of the mazes she mentioned, cheering him along until the end, then Exos stowed the mirror.

"You can have this when the trial is done," he promised her.

"I would love that," she admitted.

He kissed her on the cheek, then faced us. "All right. Thirty hours. We have our observers," he waved to the five fae who had agreed to help.

Well, maybe not all of them had agreed.

My brooding brother stood on the sidelines with his arms folded, his expression bored. He would much rather be off playing in another powerless duel. The prick had a penchant for shattering all my records. It was like he'd made it his life's mission to destroy my legacy and replace it with his own.

So yeah, I didn't feel at all bad about roping him into this assignment.

Besides, he was on probation for another month, which meant he had to do anything we told him to anyway. That was what happened when you ran off to the Human Realm to pick fights with mortals.

Honestly, Claire had gone too easy on him by just turning him into a glorified intern. He needed to serve a jail sentence for what he'd done in New York. But I respected my mate's wish to try and mentor him first. When that didn't work, I'd be pushing for a harsher sentence. He needed to learn that there were strict consequences for his actions, something I knew he didn't fully grasp yet.

"The goal here is to go about our typical day while keeping our item unharmed. But as our observers are all here at the Academy, some of us will have to improvise." Exos looked pointedly at Cyrus, as the two of them didn't reside on campus full-time. Sol, Vox, and I would be fine since we all had our respective studies. "Perhaps we can go work on the Spirit Quad? Continue the restorations?"

Cyrus nodded. "I think that would be a wise use of our time."

"I can help," Mortus replied. He was in charge of watching Exos—an activity that five years ago would have been completely off the table. We all had a history with the former Spirit Fae professor. It wasn't a good one, either. But he'd slowly redeemed himself over time, particularly via his treatment of Claire's mum, Ophelia.

The two of them had been engaged once, their third-level bonding one that should have been unbreakable. However, a bunch of shit went down that destroyed their mating and several lives.

There was a lot of heartbreak involved, but the pair seemed to be healing together.

"I guess I'll help as well," Lance muttered. "Since I'm *observing* Cyrus."

The Water Fae King made a noise through his nose. "I'm going to put you to work for that comment."

"You sound so disappointed about that," my brother drawled, his attitude problem firmly in place.

I considered saying something but decided against it. Cyrus had this sorted and would quickly put the rebellious Fire Fae in his place.

I looked at Kalt. "Guess you're joining me in the gym."

The Water Fae lit up. "I like where this is going."

"It's not all that exciting. He doesn't fight anymore," my brother replied. "You'll be bored in five minutes."

I narrowed my gaze at my hotheaded little brother. "Watch yourself."

"Or what?" He arched an auburn brow that looked exactly like my own. "You'll challenge me? Oh, wait, you're out of shape and old. So I guess you'll just stand there and spew words at me instead."

I growled, and Exos stepped in between us. "Stop baiting your brother." Royal power flared around him as he stared my brother down. "And get your ass to the Spirit Quad before I show you how I duel. And it won't be powerless."

"I don't need you to stand up for me," I muttered, irritated that he'd defused the situation using his Spirit Fae King presence.

That felt like cheating, and I didn't cheat.

"I'm not standing up for you," Exos replied, glancing over his shoulder at me. "I'm protecting our objects, which is the whole point of this exercise. If you two blow up in an inferno, it'll defeat the purpose of this test."

Well, he had me there.

I dipped my chin in subtle acknowledgment, then looked at Kalt. For whatever reason, this guy decided to be best friends with my moody brother. I'd never understand it. But I caught him giving Lance a look now that told him to cool it. My brother just rolled his eyes and turned toward the Spirit Quad with Mortus, Exos, and Cyrus following.

Vox smiled at Ophelia, then guided her toward the Air Quad, where he had classes to lead today.

Sol nodded at River—a Water Fae and my best mate from the Academy—and led him toward the Earth Quad to go help with some classes.

And I started toward the neutral campus area with Kalt. Only, after a few steps, I realized we'd forgotten an important piece.

No, not just important, but the key piece to all of this.

Our queen.

I turned to find Claire looking off in each direction, nibbling her lip. "Come join us in intramural class, sweetheart," I said softly. "We can play a game of Fae Ball."

Her blue eyes lit up at the prospect. "I haven't played that since our Academy days."

"Then let's go relive the experience. Afterward, we can spar a little."

She wasn't pregnant yet, which meant playing was absolutely allowed. And the way her face beamed at me said it was the right approach.

I wrapped an arm around her while my other hand cradled the Firebird egg.

This trial would be easy as fae pie.

And soon, Claire would be growing with my child.

I couldn't fucking wait.

CLAIRE

THE BED WAS cold without my mates, making me pleased this series of trials was coming to an end.

"They really are something," my mom murmured, observing my mates from the kitchen window. They all stood outside discussing their kitchen assignments.

Titus appeared disgruntled over something. Sol looked half-awake. Vox's expression held a touch of arrogance—as the main chef of our mate-circle, he totally had this task in the bag, and he knew it. Meanwhile, Exos and Cyrus looked just like they did thirty hours ago: handsome, polished, and ready to win.

We were waiting on Lance and Kalt, who had taken the night shift to observe and were napping through the morning hours while my mom, Mortus, and River took over.

The utter devotion to these trials warmed my heart. If I had any reservations about having a baby before, they were gone now. Because I realized how much support I had, not just from my mates but also from our family and friends.

"I'm ready," I told my mom. "I'm really ready."

"I know you are," she replied, smiling softly. "You're

going to be an amazing mom, and those mates of yours are going to make great dads."

I smiled. "Yeah, they really..." I trailed off as a swirl of flames danced along the field, heading directly for Titus. My elements engaged to throw up a shield, only my fire mate triggered his first, blasting off a wave of power in the direction of the source.

Lance.

"Ah, hell," I muttered, going to the door to stop the two hotheaded males from battling in the front yard. *Again.*

The last time this happened, they destroyed two of Sol's trees and blew out the windows to the house. Vox had been furious about all the glass, while my Earth Fae mate had threatened to bury Lance alive beneath the replacement roots.

Cyrus sighed audibly as I stepped outside, his hand forming a wall of water that protected himself and my other mates.

"That's not going to stop him," Titus muttered, a ball of fire ready in his palm.

"What's his fucking problem?" Exos demanded.

"He values his beauty rest," Titus drawled.

Cyrus snorted. "Don't we all?"

Kalt created a door and stepped through the water without getting a drop on him, while Lance sprinted through the tidal wave and directly into Exos.

Who proceeded to drop his mirror.

It shattered all over the ground, destroying his object and eliciting gasps from the group.

Exos stared at it for a moment, shock evident in his expression, then he narrowed his gaze at the cause of the issue. Titus immediately stepped in between his little brother and my Spirit Fae mate. "Apologize," he demanded, his focus on Lance. "*Now.*"

"An apology isn't going to fix my mirror," Exos muttered, his fury and sadness swirling through our bond. He'd lost the trial and he knew it, which meant he was now disqualified from the results.

All because Titus's brother had lost his temper over Fae knew what.

Shit.

"I… I'm sorry," Lance said, sounding more contrite than I'd ever heard him. Likely because he'd just pissed off the Spirit Fae King—a male known for his warrior abilities and no-nonsense attitude. "I just wanted… to fuck with… Titus."

My fire mate snorted. "Yeah, well, good job."

"I'm sorry," Lance repeated. "I didn't get a lot of sleep, and it seemed like a good way to burn off my mood. I had no idea it would… that I would… that this would…"

"It's fine," Exos said, his tone surprisingly soft. "The goal of the exercise was to protect and nurture our items. It's my failure, not yours. And it's not going to stop us from finishing this. Let's go inside. We have meals to prepare." His sapphire gaze met mine as he turned around, his sorrow echoed in the depths of his eyes. I caught through our bond that it wasn't so much disappointment of his loss as it was sadness over failing me and his object.

You're going to be an amazing father, I whispered into his mind. *And you just proved that by not losing your temper with Lance.*

He didn't mean to run into me, Exos replied. *There's no sense in being angry with him. It would just make him feel worse and doesn't solve the problem. The damage is already done.*

I know, I agreed, pressing my palm to his cheek and kissing him on the mouth. *But that reaction is what will make you a good dad. It shows patience, something your trials didn't factor in at all.*

"Exos still earns points for the nurturing trial," I decided out loud, making sure everyone knew my stance.

"Yes, accidents happen. It's how we react that matters," Cyrus echoed.

The others all murmured their agreement, my mates coming through for each other despite the competitive atmosphere.

I glanced at my mom, her eyes beaming with pride. Our relationship had been a bit rocky at first, but we'd grown closer over the years. She offered maternal guidance that was missing for most of my life. Not that my grandparents weren't great to me as a child, but they only prepared me for the human world, not the fae realms.

My mom came up to me as my mates headed inside, her hand grasping my shoulder. "You're definitely ready," she whispered, agreeing with my statement from earlier. "All of you are."

I smiled. "They're really great, aren't they?"

"They are," she agreed, heading in after them.

Kalt, Mortus, and River all followed in silence, but Lance stood just outside, his cheeks pink with chagrin. "I'm sorry, Claire."

"Water under the bridge," I replied.

He frowned. "Is that…? Are you telling me my punishment?"

I blinked at him. "No. It's a saying."

"I don't get it."

"It's a way of saying I forgive you and it's forgotten."

"What do water and a bridge have to do with

forgiveness?" he asked seriously, his green eyes the same color as his older brother's.

"It's a human phrase," I replied. "And… I actually don't know where it comes from."

"Oh." His brow furrowed. "I'll have to look that one up on my next visit."

"There won't be a next visit if you keep doing stupid things like attacking your brother with fire for no reason," I replied.

"I was playing."

"You were provoking," I corrected. "I've spent the last six months with you, Lance. I know your tells."

His lips twisted to the side. "Okay. Fine. I was bored and wanted to spar. You and Kalt got to practice all day yesterday, while I helped Cyrus reconstruct stones." He grumbled the words and rolled his eyes. "I belong in the ring, Claire."

"All you *know* is the ring and how to fight," I corrected. "The whole point of your probation is to learn about other opportunities. You're a powerful fae. There's a lot more to the realms than fighting, Lance."

He stared at me for a long moment. "I want to do something with humans. I want to find what makes them so… resilient."

Given the human fighting ring he'd played in while in New York, that admission didn't surprise me. "Then consider joining the Interrealm Fae Council initiative," I suggested. "There are a lot of opportunities there to work with others on how to hide our worlds and assimilate with humankind, too. And when the academy is up and running, maybe you can teach classes similar to Titus's, but for all fae."

His green eyes brightened. "You think I could do something like that?"

"I do," I replied, smiling at his excitement. "But you have to learn and earn it. Just like Kalt is doing now with his internship."

Some of his happiness ebbed. "I don't want to be a politician or an emissary."

"You don't have to do that; his role is only one example. Maybe you can join us at the next Interrealm Fae Council meeting to learn about other opportunities."

He considered it for a moment, then nodded. "I would like that."

"Good." I grinned. "Now let's go see what Titus plans to make. I'm guessing it's breakfast related." My mate knew how to make a killer omelet.

"Domestic Titus entertains me immensely," Lance admitted.

"It entertains me, too." But for very different reasons.

I turned to find Cyrus's eyes on me, his icy irises swirling with warmth. *I think you just showed all of us up in this nurturing trial, little queen,* he whispered into my mind.

He just needs someone to talk to, I replied. *I'm happy to be that person for him.*

It's more than that, Claire. He admires you. Not as a mate, but as a role model. And that's what he desperately needs.

He could use Titus for that, I pointed out.

He's too stubborn for it, and so is your fire mate, he replied as Exos handed him some ingredients. The two of them appeared to be cooking together rather than individually.

Vox had gone solo, making something with eggs.

Titus was working on an omelet, just like I'd thought, so they shared a space but prepared separately.

And Sol... appeared to be taking a nap at the table.

I eyed him with an arched brow. *Sol?*

Mmm? he hummed back at me.

What are you cooking? I wondered, amused by his sleepy-mind mumble.

Skittle snacks, he said, not moving an inch from the table.

Skittle snacks? I repeated, entertained. *So you found the rainbow in the Human Realm?*

Rainbow? he sounded exhausted. *I don't know about a rainbow.*

And I don't know what skittle snacks are.

Scuttle... scuttle... butt... snacks? He was full-on drifting now. Rather than wake him up, I just walked over to run my fingers through his hair and sat beside him on the bench. He snored while the others cooked.

River just chuckled and shook his head. "Well, he's not going to win."

"They all win," I murmured, stroking my earth mate's cheek. "The baby will belong to all of us, regardless of who gains the most points."

Cyrus winked at me from the kitchen, his agreement warming our bond. Exos handed him a plate of chopped vegetables, which my water mate proceeded to layer into a casserole dish.

"Where the fuck is my Firebird egg?" Titus suddenly demanded, causing Sol to jolt awake beside me. His forehead had a bunch of crispy flakes embedded into it from the table. He narrowed his eyes, then flicked the items from his head and onto the table in a confetti-like confusion.

"Oh..." Vox turned beet red, his eyes widening. "Uh..."

"You didn't." Titus stared down my air mate, their similar heights making them eye level with each other. But Titus had about thirty pounds more muscle on him than Vox. "Tell me you didn't *cook my Firebird egg.*"

"Did you put it on the counter?" Vox asked, his voice lifting at the end into a squeak.

"I told you I did!"

"I... I didn't remember... I was in my groove... and..."

"You cooked my fucking egg." Titus threw his spatula down on a growl and gripped his auburn locks in his fists. "Fuckin' fires, Vox!"

"I'm sorry!" my air mate exclaimed.

Cyrus and Exos just shook their heads, chuckling as they continued their own dishes.

Sol munched on his ingredients beside me, completely forgetting the point of this exercise as we watched the battle in the kitchen unfold.

Vox's eggs went up in flames, causing him to engage his air magic to try to put out the fire. But Titus was raging and completely lost to his annoyance.

Not exactly a nurturing reaction, but I understood his frustration. They hadn't slept in thirty hours, and he'd been on his way to winning the trials. While I meant what I said about us all winning, I knew Titus had a competitive edge from his time in the Powerless Champion ring.

He eventually calmed down after a few minutes, resigned to his fate, and finished his omelet while Vox scraped his burnt eggs into the trash with a scowl.

Sol chuckled, nearly halfway done with whatever the hell he was supposed to make. He offered me a few berries, which I took and popped into my mouth.

Then his brow furrowed, and the light bulb went off. "Ah, hell."

I giggled and took more of his berries. "Tastes great, Sol."

He grumbled and picked up his peach for a bite before holding it out to me. "Might as well enjoy it."

"Are you suggesting we eat our future children?"

He snorted. "It's juicy and ripe. Take a bite. I already lost anyway."

"None of us are losing anything," I reminded him before indulging in a taste. He was right about the ripeness. It was perfection and made me groan in approval. He licked the juice off my lips, then fed me another bite, his disappointment over failing his trials disappearing in a blink. Sol never stayed upset for long.

He licked more peach juice off my lips, then slipped his tongue into my mouth for a long, sensuous kiss. I momentarily forgot we had an audience until River cleared his throat. "While your mom is aware of the purpose of these trials, I don't think she wants to witness the consummation."

Warmth touched my cheeks as I pulled away from Sol to find my mother and Mortus intently watching Exos and Cyrus finish their casserole dish. The pink tinge in my mother's cheeks told me she'd definitely seen my kiss with Sol and had likely overheard River's commentary.

I cleared my throat and tried my best to keep my hands to myself.

Your vagina still broken, little queen? Cyrus asked as he slid the casserole into the oven. *Or are you ready for more orgasms?*

I swallowed. *I... I feel better; thank you for asking.*

His silver-blue eyes found mine. *Good. Because I intend to bend you over that table in a few hours.*

The heat in my cheeks spread down my breasts, my body warming to the idea of his touch. *You assume you've won.*

I know I have, he replied, leaning against the counter and holding my gaze. *And you know I have, too.*

He was right.

I knew he'd won as well.

If I were honest, I'd say he won before all of this had started. He always considered every angle and outcome before engaging in a challenge, and I'd never seen him lose. Not even to Titus when they dueled. At best, they would call it a draw.

That's why Exos didn't get mad; he already knew you were going to win.

Yes, Cyrus agreed. *But also, he knew Lance didn't mean it. Getting mad at him would only worsen the issue, not fix it.*

That's pretty much what Exos said, I replied.

That doesn't surprise me at all, little queen.

It didn't surprise me either. Cyrus and Exos were a lot alike. Not just because they were brothers, but because they were both kings. It required a certain amount of patience and understanding to act as the conduits for their elements.

I relaxed into Sol's side as my mates cleaned up in the kitchen.

Then I waited as they presented their dishes.

Vox didn't have one because he'd tossed it into the trash.

Titus gave me an omelet with all my favorite ingredients—I shared it with everyone else for the taste test, and the others agreed it was well done.

Then Exos and Cyrus presented their leafy casserole. It reminded me of a shepherd's pie without the meat.

No one commented on the fact that they'd worked together on it, mostly because it was a demonstration of our future. We had to work as a team. It was the best way to raise our future child.

No. Not child. *Children.*

Because seeing them all now, I realized I wanted more than one. I needed to have them all. One for every element. I felt the truth of it deep inside—the desire to create as much life as we could.

Perhaps not right away, but over time.

And I would start with Cyrus.

Everyone agreed that he'd won. He didn't gloat so much as accept the responsibility with pride. Then he gazed meaningfully at me, and the others left the room.

Not my mates, but the observers.

I barely felt them leave, my focus entirely on my water mate and the intentions warming the air between us.

"It's Halloween, Claire," he said, prowling toward me. "How do you want to celebrate?"

"By trick-or-treating?" I suggested.

His lips curled. "How about we skip the trick part and get right to the treat?" He grabbed my hips and pulled me up onto the counter of the kitchen. "We'll indulge in your sweetness first. Then you can indulge in ours."

"We?" I repeated on a breath. "Ours?"

"You didn't think I'd leave them out of our conception night, did you?" he asked, his hands sliding up my thighs and beneath my skirt, pushing it to my hips. "We're a mate-circle, little queen. I might be the one planting my seed tonight, but you can bet we're all going to be inside you in some way."

My heart skipped a beat. "None of you have slept."

"We don't need sleep to properly fuck you," he countered, his lips sealing over mine. "Now lie down. It's our turn to eat."

CYRUS

CLAIRE'S BODY glistened with sex, her drowsy gaze catching mine as she lounged like some sort of erotic offering on the bed between all her mates.

I'd tasted her first, giving her a quick orgasm with my tongue before I stepped back and allowed the others to prepare her. Her comments regarding her broken insides were long erased by hours of proof to the contrary.

Now she beckoned me with a sweet smile, aware of what I intended to do next.

Exos sucked her nipple into his mouth while Vox laved her other tit.

Titus licked between her legs while Sol combed his fingers through her hair, his lips reverent as he kissed her temple, her forehead, and then her lips.

But as he pulled away, I found her gaze again, the heated orbs an invitation.

She was ready.

And so was I.

You're overdressed, she murmured into my mind.

Am I? I began unknotting my tie. *Perhaps you should help me out of my clothes, little queen.*

Titus chose that moment to draw his teeth over her clit, causing her to jolt and shoot flames from her fingertips. I caught them in a glove of water, extinguishing the burn, and created a mist around us that set the tone for our joining.

We'd moved Claire from the kitchen to our bedroom hours ago, the entire floor a mattress made for our weekly gatherings.

The windows were covered in curtains. Vines and flowers decorated the wall. And the ceiling was enchanted by spirit magic, the winking lights reminding me of stars.

Claire writhed beneath it all, her moans music to my ears. I tossed my tie to the pile of clothes in the corner and kicked off my shoes and socks. My mate watched with lazy anticipation, her pupils dilated with desire.

She murmured something through her bonds to the other males, causing them to back away just enough for her to kneel before me. My lips curled at the wantonness playing over her gorgeous features.

I knew what she intended.

And there wasn't a chance in hell I was about to stop her.

She grabbed my belt and threaded it through the loops before dropping it at her side. Then she grasped my button-down shirt and yanked it out of my slacks to expose my lower abdomen. Her lips met my skin, lighting my being on fire from that touch alone.

My dick pulsed in response, ready to play.

But I let her take her time, exploring me with her tongue as she slowly unfastened my pants and pulled down the zipper.

A subtle push sent them down my legs, followed by my boxers as she freed my cock to her mouth.

She didn't ask or comment, just took my throbbing

head into her mouth and swallowed me down as far as her throat allowed.

"Fuck, Claire," I groaned, fisting my fingers in her hair. "Do that again and I won't have anything left to give you."

Her blue eyes flared as she met my gaze, her cheeks hollowing around my shaft in a delicious caress that nearly sent me to my knees.

This woman sucked cock like no one else.

And I would happily die in this position.

Because *fuck*.

It was so intense, so beautiful, so damn perfect that I almost wept. Instead, I praised her with my thoughts and drew my fingers through her hair, thanking her for the gift of her alluring mouth.

She swallowed me again, her tongue masterful against my skin, then she released me with a pop. I almost growled a protest, but her fingers hooked into my shirt and tugged me down to her on the mattress. I chuckled as I landed on top of her, which I suspected was exactly what she desired.

Rather than remove my shirt, she set it on fire and burned it away from my skin. I could have stopped her, but I didn't want to. My mate's penchant for destroying clothes intrigued me. Although, it was proving to be a costly little hobby of hers. Most of my suits were from the Human Realm, all handmade and tailored in Italy. Same with Exos's.

Not that Claire cared about the semantics of our wardrobe.

Our little queen just wanted us naked and inside her, which was exactly what I gave her by spreading her thighs beneath me and sliding home without an ounce of foreplay.

Her body was already primed and ready, thanks to her other mates. She didn't need my hands or tongue. What she required was my cock, and that was precisely what I gave her as she wrapped her legs around my waist and urged me to fuck her.

I kissed her hard, palming her neck to angle her where I wanted. My other hand went to her tit, giving it a squeeze for her attempt at taking control.

She grinned against my mouth. *You're not mad.*

Never, I agreed. *I love the way you play with me, little queen. It makes this so much more enjoyable.*

I drove into her, smiling at her responding moan.

How many orgasms have you had tonight? I asked her. *Seven?*

Yes, she hissed, arching into me.

Are we going for eight or nine? I wondered, my lips leaving hers to trail down her throat to her flushed breasts. Fuck, she was a sight to behold, all wicked lust and salacious intent.

The men around me agreed, their cocks all stirring at the thought of fucking her again.

She made us insatiable beasts, with her as our queen at the center of this dark madness.

But I had a role to perform tonight, one Claire would need to play an equal part in for it to take.

I kissed her again, muting whatever reply stirred in her thoughts, her mind and body protesting the idea of nine orgasms in a night. Ridiculous, because we all knew she could handle so much more.

Fae—no matter our origin or kingdom—were beings of life and creation. We craved sex.

Even though she was half-human, her fae side overrode her where it counted, making her close to immortal and capable of endless hours—or days—of pleasure.

I reminded her of that with my mouth and cock, spearing her, owning her, driving her to the brink of rapture by hitting that spot deep inside.

She soared for me.

Screamed.

Her cheeks red with the force of pleasure overtaking her being.

I nuzzled her throat, slowing my pace, readying her for what would come next.

A new bond of sorts.

The heart of fae magic.

She whimpered, her over-sensitized body rippling with aftershocks of her ecstasy. Her mind was already protesting again, but I shushed her with a gentle kiss, my movements below measured and deliberate.

"Are you ready to make a baby, little queen?" I murmured against her mouth.

Warmth blossomed all around us from the others, their hands reaching out to stroke her in their own ways. Sol fondled her hair. Exos touched the side of her breast, stroking downward. Titus kissed her hip, his palm drifting from my backside to her thigh. And Vox drew his finger along her arm.

They were all here, all ready, all focused on the heart of our mate-circle.

Claire's thick blonde lashes fluttered open, her gaze gleaming with approval. "Yes. I'm ready."

I kissed her tenderly, my heart skipping a beat at the perfection of this moment. In a previous life, I never would have imagined this possible. Now, I couldn't picture it any other way.

Claire was the love of my life, the only one I would ever want. But I cherished her other mates as well, loving them all in their own ways. It was as if our elements all thrived as a hive unit, because of Claire as our core and conduit.

She was our version of the elemental source.

Our goddess.

Our queen.

And it was finally time to create new life inside her.

I slid out all the way to the tip, before plunging deep and awakening her pleasure once more. She groaned, her back bowing as she encouraged me to do it again.

I did.

But this time, I reached into our shared element as well.

Her eyes widened, feeling the power rippling over us as I called forth my water magic to bind us together as one. To *create*.

She shivered, her connection to the element opening wide in response as she matched my swirling wave with one of her own, bathing in our shared power, marrying it together as one.

The others could feel it, their skin misting as a result.

But the true source of the element coated me and Claire, swathing us in a sea of familiar bliss.

I kissed her, reveling in the sensation of our element playing through our beings, engaging our souls, and warming with the gift of life.

All it takes is a thought, I whispered to her. *Accept my offering, Claire.*

She didn't ask what I meant, because she felt the warmth of my power brushing her soul. She opened beneath it, gasping as the element pierced her very heart, sending vibrant electricity through her veins and mine.

It centered in my groin, alighting me from within

and stirring a cyclone of sensation in my lower abdomen. I growled from the onslaught, the pleasure unlike anything I'd ever experienced, even during our first mating.

Fae are meant to create, I thought at her. *Fuck, Claire. I can't hold back much longer.*

It was too intense.

Too overpowering.

Too *right*.

She squeezed me with her thighs, welcoming me into her body with little movements of her own, the sensation curling inside her as well. I could feel it through our bond, her acceptance and excitement. Her preparedness. Her *need*.

Her limbs began to shake, sexy noises falling from her lips, as she picked up the pace of our joining, forcing me to shoot off into an oblivion of stars. Water exploded around us, my control over the element snapping as I released my seed inside her on a roar of emotion and astute gratification.

Claire followed me with her own scream, her nails digging into my back as she held on through each rapturous wave of insanity.

I couldn't breathe.

We were drowning in my element, lost in the depths of the ocean and struggling to surface. I held on to her as she clung to me, our lungs failing us both.

Until we surfaced on a collective breath, our lips crashing into each other as we mated our tongues in a dark dance of fate and expectation.

I fucking loved this woman.

She took everything I had to give and gave it back tenfold, her body a pillar of worship that I would forever kneel to.

And inside, life had taken hold.

I could feel it in my very being, the source rejoicing in our mating and showering us in icy kisses that stung my already damp skin. Claire giggled, her smile the most beautiful sight.

Rather than speak, she kissed me again. Then she grabbed Sol and dragged him in for a kiss. Followed by Titus, Vox, and then Exos.

I was still joined to her below, could feel her walls fluttering with renewed vigor, her happiness a drug we all wanted to indulge in.

My hips flexed, giving her what she craved.

We'd already created life, but I didn't mind fucking her again. Just as I knew her mates wouldn't mind joining.

Now it was about celebrating. Worshipping. Cherishing. Existing.

Our Claire had just given us all the biggest gift of our lives. And we intended to show her our gratitude for as long as she wanted.

Thank you, little queen, I whispered, kissing her jaw as Sol took her mouth again. *I love you,* I added, palming her belly. *Both of you.*

PART TWO

'Tis The Season To Be Pregnant Fa-la-la-la-la La-la La La

CLAIRE

TEN DAYS LATER

"CLAIRE!" Titus shouted, making my eyebrows scrunch as I pulled the blanket over my head. He shook me, albeit gently, as he insisted on rousing me from the best sleep of my life. When I didn't respond, he pulled the sheets away, making me squirm as cool air rushed over my skin.

"So tired," I mumbled as I tried to fend him off with a wave of my hand. "Go away."

"Thank the source you're finally awake," he said on an exhale. I peeked at him with one eye, finding him leaning back on his heels as he watched me. "How... how are you feeling?"

A blanket of fatigue draped over me in response to his question, refusing to lift its weight entirely, but the concern in Titus's eyes made me sit up.

"What time is it?" I asked, confused. Sunlight streamed in with pleasant rays that banished the strange chill in the room, but it felt like no time had passed at all since I'd laid my head down.

He rubbed the back of his neck. "Uh, it's midday."

He continued to stare at me, his eyes running over me as if he was searching for a source of injury.

"What is it?" I asked. "Why are you looking at me like that?"

"Because you slept much longer than I expected."

I raised an eyebrow at him. It wasn't like I hadn't ever slept in before. "And that concerns you... why?"

He sighed and took my hand, warming me with his magic. I jolted at the unforgiving warmth, frowning. "Because you're pregnant, Claire. It's my job to be concerned."

Yes, I was pregnant, and just the affirmation in my mind made my heart flutter with joy. There could be no denying the surge of life I'd felt through my bond with Cyrus and all of my mates.

"Is the faeling doing okay?" he asked after a moment, as if it was something I should have confirmed already.

"What?"

"The faeling," he said again, his words coming out in that slow, calm way when I knew he was starting to worry. "Can you feel it?"

I frowned. "Should I be able to?" Could he not feel the life thriving through the bond? It seemed pretty real to me. But maybe I was mistaking it for something else?

He stilled for a moment, as though trying too hard not to show a reaction. "Exos didn't think we should prod you about it, but now that you've passed the incubation period, you should be able to feel something."

I wasn't sure exactly what Titus meant by that, but it unfurled a thread of doubt that this pregnancy would take hold. I knew that Cyrus had filled me with life, but this was a fae mating.

And I was only half-fae.

It was a secret, dark fear I hadn't considered until it jolted through me with ugly clarity. As a Halfling, I didn't quite fit in either world. It was my mates who had made a place for me. To everyone else, I was just an oddity…

An abomination.

What if that meant I couldn't procreate? What if I'd been too lost in my mates' love for me that I'd missed the dreadful truth right in front of me?

"Maybe we shouldn't get our hopes up, Titus," I said, warning him with a slight tremor in my voice. I really didn't want my mates to be disappointed if my human half took charge in this instance. Even if this pregnancy failed, it didn't mean I would stop trying. When he continued to frown at me, I added, "We don't know if the pregnancy is, uh, viable."

"Viable?" he repeated, his hand drifting to my shoulder. "Do you not remember Cyrus and you conceiving? Or are you doubting him?" The latter question seeped with hurt, but he misunderstood my concern. I didn't doubt my mates so much as I doubted myself.

I brushed off his touch as another wave of fatigue wafted over me. I covered my mouth and yawned. "It's only been a little over a week since we, um, since we tried, I mean."

I rubbed my eyes, part of me wanting to throw the covers over my head again and just go back to sleep and hide from all my doubts and fears.

"It'll be at least a month before we know anything for certain. And even then, we're supposed to wait a bit before we really start planning. I don't actually know the statistics, but miscarriages sometimes happen in humans." It was a male-fae bonus to have control over conception, but I wasn't exactly a textbook case.

Titus cocked his brow. "Miscarriage?" He shook his head. "We'll know in a lot less than a month, Claire. And I think you underestimate your genetics and the potency of male fae." He grinned. "Especially a male like your Water King, who is even cockier than me. He has a reputation to uphold, you know."

I sighed. Cyrus's virility wasn't what I questioned. "You're not hearing me." I really didn't know how to explain this without the fissure in my heart splitting open.

What if I failed my mates?

What if I was broken?

"Hey." Titus leaned in so that I could see his green eyes blazing with heat. "I *am* hearing you, sweetheart, and I'm telling you that you have nothing to worry about. You know why?" He grazed his fingers over my chin, making me sink into his touch.

"Why?" I asked, my voice hopeful even though my stomach twisted with worry.

"Because you are life itself, Claire." His smile lifted into a smirk. "And there's no way you'd fall asleep during sex unless you had a good excuse, so if you *aren't* pregnant, I'm afraid I can't forgive you for that."

I frowned. "What?" I'd passed out during sex before —because a girl can only take so many orgasms before her brain just shuts down—but falling asleep? That wasn't possible. "There's no way..." I trailed off.

He chuckled. "Tell me the last thing you remember."

"We were playing with fire," I said slowly, recalling how he'd been agonizing me with slow flames that ran up the insides of my thighs. "Then..." My words drifted off as I tried to remember what happened next. The warmth and excitement were there, but my memories sort of just... stopped.

"You fell asleep," he finished for me.

I frowned, then gasped when I realized he was right. "Oh, Titus," I said, covering my mouth, "I'm so sorry!"

He laughed. "It's a good sign, sweetheart. The first month of fae pregnancy comes with extreme fatigue because the baby has a lot of growing to do in a short amount of time. You're going to sleep a lot, especially during the incubation period. Although, you had me worried with how much sleep you needed."

He enveloped me in an embrace, coddling me as if I were made of porcelain. He also seemed to think that saying things like "incubation period" was completely normal.

"I'm glad you're comfortable enough to trust me with your protection. Fae instincts tend to keep the mother awake until she feels it's safe." He gave me another gentle hug before releasing me. "Now that you're past the first phase, I'll go find the Healer. We're going to need to have you checked out for phase two."

The authority in his voice said "no" would not be an acceptable answer.

I blinked a few times, not sure what he meant by "phase one" and "phase two" or why he kept saying I was incubating like I was some sort of damned chicken.

My hand went to my belly while Titus rolled off the bed and grabbed his clothes.

"Shouldn't we do a pregnancy test or something first?" I asked. That would at least confirm the pregnancy, right?

He chuckled. "A test? What do you mean?"

I bit my lip before replying. "You know, it involves peeing on a stick?"

He stumbled midstride as he looped one pant leg over his foot. "Excuse me?"

Exasperated, I let my hands fall to the sheets. "How do fae know if they're pregnant? In my world, you pee on a stick, and it tells you a positive or a negative result."

He barked out a laugh. "Humans have such odd magic. No, you don't pee on a stick, Claire. You can tell if you're pregnant with your elements. Use the spirit source." When I stared at him, he continued. "Have you tried it?"

I swallowed past the lump in my throat. Reaching into myself to touch the elemental sources was second nature, but when I tried to touch the spirit source, nothing happened.

"I don't feel anything," I said, starting to worry. "Does that mean the baby…?"

Titus went still, and a brief moment of seriousness swept over his features. It passed, replaced with his usual sexy smirk as he finished getting dressed. "I'm sure everything's fine. You're a Halfling, so that could be impacting the connection to the source during pregnancy. This will be a new experience for everyone, so let's just take it one step at a time, okay?"

I tried not to hyperventilate.

Or it means something's wrong.

What if I really had miscarried?

"Do Halflings usually have faelings?" I asked, starting to panic. "Is it normal for us… to…? Do you know of one who has? What if… what if…?" I swallowed the lump in my throat and palmed my belly, a sense of protectiveness sweeping over me.

I desperately clung to Titus's speculation that my child might impact my connection to the source. Anything more sinister than that and I would be sick.

"Just breathe, sweetheart," Titus said, his voice a calming presence in my mind, drawing me back to him and out of the shadows of my concerns. "Let's meet with the Healer, okay? She'll tell you what to expect."

Yes. Okay. He was right. "A Healer," I repeated. "That sounds… that sounds good."

He gave me a kiss on the cheek, reassuring me with a graze of magical warmth. "Everything's going to be fine," he repeated, perhaps saying it more for his benefit than mine. He gave my arm a light squeeze before he ventured out the door. "I'll be back in a few minutes, Claire. Just relax."

Relax, I repeated to myself. *Yeah, sure.*

But I tried anyway, releasing a long breath.

Where are you guys? I asked through the bonds.

The guys all answered quickly. Cyrus was out rounding up appropriate fae willing to meet with me about the Interrealm Fae Academy. Exos, Sol, and Vox were all out in the Human Realm procuring decorations for the holidays. Something about wanting to decorate my office—an idea that made me smile. That explained some of the random bags in the bedroom, all overflowing with autumn colors and a few with red and green.

Is everything going okay? I asked Cyrus.

I should be asking you that, little queen, he replied, his voice a kiss against my thoughts. *And yes, everything's fine. Kalt is helping me, too. I think he's avoiding his triad issue with the Winter Fae.*

I really want to know more about that, I admitted.

Me, too. I'll see what I can learn and report back. He sounded amused. *I'll be there soon, little queen. And don't worry; you are definitely pregnant.*

I frowned. *Are you playing in my head?*

No, your concern is radiating through the bond. Your fae

genetics trump your human half. Trust me, he murmured. *We're all heading back for your Healer appointment, little queen.*

He left me with a misty kiss to my mind, his focus returning to his tasks.

Thank you, I whispered back to him. It wouldn't be easy to convince the other fae to create the Interrealm Fae Academy, which was why I wanted to meet with them all individually, to assure them their needs would be met. And there was no one better to convince them than my Water Fae King mate. He wouldn't take "no" for an answer.

Sighing, I jumped out of the bed and hurried to the shower. I felt kind of grimy for some reason. Maybe because I'd slept for too long? Yet, I could easily sleep more right now.

To banish my lingering fatigue, I made the shower cold, which seemed to do the trick.

After I finished, I studied myself in the mirror as water dripped from my long blonde locks. My breasts looked the same as usual, perky and ready for my mates' attention. Although, as I ran my hands over them, my nipples did feel a little sore. My fingers ran down, circling the belly button on my flat abdomen.

I tried to access the spirit source again, only to find a sense of nothingness. It wasn't as if the space inside of me felt empty—rather, it felt blocked.

Hmm. I wasn't sure what to make of that.

Running my fingers through my wet hair, I reached for the fire source out of habit to dry the dripping strands.

And nothing happened.

My stomach sank as I paused, then tried again.

Drip. Drip. Drip.

Water hit the floor, mocking me at my attempt to

touch the fire source, which worked great as a magical dryer.

Frowning, I decided not to panic. Maybe Titus was right. I was a Halfling, and being pregnant could have strange effects on my powers. If I couldn't access the spirit source, it made sense that I wouldn't be able to access the others as well. Although, I didn't like the sensation of helplessness that came with feeling so... *human*.

"Well, if you're going to be human, then you might as well act the part," I said to myself, leaning on the counter to make sure my reflection heard my determination.

I didn't have a human hair dryer, so I snatched up a towel and scrubbed until my hair went from soaking wet to damp. I plaited the strands into a complex braid, wrapping it around my head like a crown. The style was popular with the Water Fae, who preferred to leave their hair wet. I had learned it from one of the students —Artica.

That done, I put on a loose-fitting blouse and matched it with a blue skirt that complemented my eyes. I didn't allow myself to linger or let my thoughts drift. I propped my hands on my hips and surveyed my bedroom filled with decorations.

Yes, a distraction would suit me well.

CLAIRE

I SEPARATED the decorations into piles based on theme.

Halloween—even though it had already passed. However, Exos liked the skeletons.

Autumn Solstice to represent the fae.

Then Christmas and Winter Solstice decorations made up the third pile. Christmas was just around the corner—plus it was my favorite of all the holidays—so I liked to start sneaking in hints of tinsel and garland wherever possible.

I started wrapping the pumpkin lights around one of the pillars in the living room, then took to the other with one of the Christmas silver stars. I finished off the third and fourth with standard fae lights, although they were more like dull orbs since I couldn't access my magic to activate them.

A problem to deal with, um, later.

I had nearly finished up with the kitchen when Titus, Cyrus, and an unknown fae walked in. They all stopped in their tracks and openly gaped at me. I'd just scrambled up the countertop to put the finishing touch on the room. I'd dragged a massive red ribbon in tow, determined to affix it to the arch that ran along the ceiling above the stove.

"Claire!" Cyrus shouted, his tone panicked. "Get down immediately!"

Ignoring him, I kicked off my shoe and hooked my toes into one of the unused shelves, gaining a bit more height. "I've almost got it," I insisted out loud. "I survived the end of the world. I can survive tying up a bow."

"Vox!" he yelled, turning to the Air Fae, who had just walked in with Sol on his heels. "Help me get her down."

Titus rubbed his temples. "Will someone talk some sense into her before we yank her down with Vox's faulty magic?"

"My magic is fine," Vox replied, glaring at the Fire Fae. His element only acted up when he became stressed or emotional—a side effect he'd never quite gotten over since mating with me. And given the panic flaying our bond, he was definitely feeling a bit emotional right now.

Exos entered last, his smirk a sharp contrast to the looks of raw panic from my other mates.

"Well, it looks like I was right," he said, sounding amused. "Claire has officially entered phase two, and the child is definitely a troublemaker." He slapped Cyrus on the back. "Well done, brother."

Vox worked a careful strand of wind magic, swirling pressure around my body to give me a lift. The extra boost of height allowed me to loop the ribbon's tassel through the slat, and I secured it before Vox guided me to the floor.

"There!" I said, slapping my hands together as I surveyed the finishing touch on my decorations. The massive red ribbon brought it all together. "Perfect."

I turned, and the smile on my face melted when I saw that my guys most certainly didn't share my festive enthusiasm, except maybe Exos, who was still pleased with himself.

The unknown fae—who I assumed was the Healer—cleared her throat. "Well, suffice it to say, I do think your mates are right. You're exhibiting all of the typical phase two traits."

I blinked, then glanced around at my still-displeased mates. "Yeah, so, will somebody explain to me what all these phases mean? Where I come from, there are three trimesters, and I'm definitely not in the second one. I'm only, like, a little over a week pregnant. That's hardly enough time for anything to happen." Not to mention there were certain concerns yet to address.

Cyrus took one of my hands and placed a kiss on my knuckles. The gesture made me soften a little. "Little queen, things are going to move fast now. Once the Healer checks you out, we really should start making preparations." He glanced around the room. "While I'm sure the faeling will appreciate a festive atmosphere, we should be focused on the nursery. We don't have a crib, clothes, or any of the items we need for a newborn."

Exos crossed his arms. "It's important to keep Claire happy. Plus, fae furniture is just fine."

I propped my hands on my hips, catching a loose strand of tinsel in my fingers. I looped it around my throat like a necklace. "We have nine months before we have to worry about any of that, so will you all just simmer down and let me celebrate the holidays?"

My guys all took on various expressions of shock. Sol went pale. Vox's mouth parted. Exos and Cyrus shared a long look, and Titus tightened his jaw.

My fire mate nudged the Healer forward. "You'd better have her sit down," he said, his voice coming out strained. "I think there's a human-slash-fae difference we all forgot to consider."

I raised an eyebrow. "Like what?"

The Healer released a nervous laugh as she took my hand and guided me into the living room. She paused, staring at the array of festive pillows shaped like Christmas ornaments before managing to clear a space for us both to sit down.

She waited until I was fully seated and all my guys had followed us into the room before she spoke. "It seems there is a key detail your mates may have failed to mention," she said, her tone scolding as she glanced at the male fae.

Cyrus folded his arms. "She's a Halfling, but she's also a queen and a goddess of the elements. Informing her of all the possibilities seems presumptuous on our parts."

I glared at him. "Presumptuous?" I turned back to the Healer. "What is it that you're trying to tell me? Is there a huge difference between fae and human pregnancies?"

The Healer gave me a weak smile as she patted my hand. "You're exhibiting all the signs of a typical fae pregnancy. There are three phases. The first is incubation, which happens while asleep. From Titus's testimony, you've already surpassed that during your three days of rest, although usually it's only twenty-four hours—"

"*Three days?*" I repeated. "I've been asleep for *three days?* When was somebody going to tell me that?"

Cyrus gave me a sympathetic smile. "We thought it best for Titus to be there when you woke up. It's normal, I assure you." He gave the Healer a nod. "Please, continue."

She cleared her throat. "Right, well, the next phase is nesting, which I would say by all the, uh, decorations, you've officially started." She turned my hand over. "May I?"

I swallowed past the lump in my throat before I nodded my permission.

She ran her palm over mine, sending a pleasant silver glow into the room. I sensed spirit magic working over me, although it felt more distant than usual. She hummed with thought, then ran her glowing hand up my arm and down over my stomach. She smiled. "Yes, you're progressing nicely."

The tension in the room eased. "So... I'm still pregnant?"

Yes, little queen, Cyrus murmured into my thoughts. *Definitely pregnant.*

The Healer laughed. "Yes, dear, and you have a healthy fae child blossoming in your womb. If no one has said it yet, congratulations."

I swayed against the wave of relief that swept over me.

I was definitely pregnant.

With Cyrus's child.

And the baby is okay.

The solace that swept through me was strong enough to make me feel giddy. "So, I'm in the second phase?" I asked, my voice wavering. I needed something practical to hold on to right now before I turned into an emotional puddle on the floor. "I'm, uh, nesting?"

She smiled and nodded. "Yes. You're preparing for your child to be born, and that means creating an environment your instincts find conducive to a relaxed and joyful ambience."

A strong gust of wind swept through the room, a

testimony to Vox's stress levels. He batted at the retaliating hanging decorations while Sol pulled out a strand of fae cherry puffs from his bag and started eating them off the string.

"Those are supposed to be hung up," I told him.

"And eaten," he agreed, inhaling another mouthful.

"I wouldn't call this relaxed," Vox said slowly, looking around at all the decorations and the mass of bags they'd just brought home with them.

I frowned. "What do you mean, this isn't relaxed?"

"It's... sort of busy?" he replied, deepening my frown.

Did he not understand the point of the holidays? "Titus?" I asked, pointing at the dull orbs wrapped around the nearest pillar. "Could you light those for me, please?"

He arched his brow but didn't ask me why I hadn't done it myself. Instead, he obeyed and flicked his fingers, sending the swirl of orbs alight. Cyrus silently activated the second one, giving the room a complement of fire and water that made my shoulders relax.

"See?" the Healer asked with a smile. "That makes you feel better, doesn't it?"

I nodded, sighing. "I've always liked decorating for the holidays. That doesn't mean anything." I leaned in. "So, you're telling me I'm past the 'incubation' period and now I'm nesting. How can I be nesting if I'm only a week pregnant?"

Well, technically, ten days since I apparently slept for three of them.

She patted my hand again, this time more forcefully. "Your pregnancy will be similar to that of a fae, not a human." She glanced at my pointed ears. They had transformed years ago after I had accepted the fae side of myself. "You've lived in the Elemental Fae realm for quite a few years now, and you have fae mates. Therefore, it makes sense for your pregnancy to run a similar course to a fae's."

I glanced around the room and found that none of my mates would meet my gaze. Finally, I zoomed back in on the Healer. "And what does that mean, exactly?" I demanded, suspecting this was the part my mates had "forgotten to mention" to me.

She chewed her lip before appeasing me. "You say that a human pregnancy lasts for nine months? Well, a fae one runs a bit shorter."

"How much shorter?" I pressed.

Cyrus took pity on me and massaged my shoulders. His gaze said that he took full responsibility for this situation, being the one who'd impregnated me. "You'll likely be delivering our child in about two months, little queen."

My entire world screeched to a halt, and my stomach dropped.

"I'm sorry… *What?*"

CYRUS

"Nine weeks." Claire repeated those two words over and over again, her feet moving swiftly over our bedroom floor as she paced back and forth.

Back and forth.

Back and forth.

"Nine weeks."

More pacing.

More mumbling.

I glanced at Exos, and he gave me a look that said, "What did you expect?"

I had expected her to understand and believe she was more fae than human. I had also expected her to be pleased that she would come to term in nine weeks, not nine months. Who would prefer nearly a year as an incubator when they could be done in roughly two months?

Of course, I wouldn't say that out loud now. Not with Claire in her tender condition. My usual go-to of pushing her to accept fate wasn't going to work this time. She might not feel it yet, but her hormones and body were already changing. Adding more stress to that transition wouldn't be helpful for either of us.

So rather than speak, I wrapped a blanket of mist around her and allowed the droplets to tease her exposed skin. She wore a cute little skirt and button-down shirt that I very much wanted to remove from her body. But something told me that would not be welcome in this state.

I also adored her hairstyle choice. It was a damp braid commonly worn by Water Fae. All she needed was her crown to fit her role as queen of my kind. She didn't wear it often, only to formal events. But I sometimes fantasized about her wearing those jewels... and only those jewels.

Something about this woman always sent my mind to my groin, which perked up with interest as she turned around to reveal her dampening shirt.

No bra.

Fuck.

Exos's sapphire gaze flashed with interest.

He'd misted back to the Water Kingdom with us. It was technically my night with Claire, and I had intended to take her to dinner with my father and his mate, but I'd postponed that dinner to brunch tomorrow. I needed to calm my little queen down first.

"Nine weeks," she said for the umpteenth time, shaking her head.

"Yes, that's roughly sixty-three days," I informed her dryly.

So much for my calm approach.

She spun to face me as though she'd forgotten I sat on our bed a few feet away. My gaze immediately dropped to her tits, those beautiful dusky nipples were completely visible beneath her shirt, and she hadn't even noticed.

Perhaps my mist blanket had been a bad idea.

But I absolutely didn't regret it as the fabric started to mold to her chest.

"*Days?*" Claire repeated.

I rolled my eyes. "Come on, little queen. Sixty-three days is plenty of time. Nine weeks. Would you prefer to be carrying around a faeling for nine months? That's an awfully long time to be pregnant, don't you think?"

Exos grunted beside me, whether in agreement or to chastise my directness, I wasn't sure. I also didn't care.

"How am I supposed to gather all the requisite approvals for the Interrealm Fae Academy in *sixty-three days?*" she demanded. "You should have told me about this before I agreed! You knew how important that academy is to me. And now there's no way I'll be able to get this done, Cyrus. I'm going to have a baby in nine weeks!"

"Technically, it'll be closer to seven now," I murmured, which was apparently the wrong thing to say, because she screamed.

I flinched.

Exos groaned.

And I recalled the warnings from the Healer about Claire's impending hormonal changes. Phase two came with a lot of physical and mental imbalances, nurturing instincts, and general nesting practices. It was the longest of the pregnancy periods and the hardest.

Phase three was the one I rather looked forward to.

But I wouldn't get into that now with her.

Instead, I focused on what her real concern was here —the Interrealm Fae Academy.

"Little queen," I said softly.

"Don't you 'little queen' me," she snapped. "*You* got me pregnant!"

I chuckled. "Indeed, I did. And I don't regret it."

Even with you yelling at me, I thought, pushing off the bed to stand in front of her. "*Little queen,*" I repeated, taking hold of her shoulders. "You have five mates."

"I'm aware, but you're the one—"

"No, Claire. That's not what I mean. You have five mates who can help you and *will* help you with the academy. We all know how important it is to you. The hard part is already done. Now we just need to arrange meetings with the fae to encourage them to agree. Do you know what Exos and I happen to be very skilled at?" I arched a brow, waiting for her to consider my words and hear what I was saying to her.

She nibbled her lip, her blue eyes flashing with consideration as she fought her instinct to rage instead of reason with me. "You… you like politics."

"Yes," I replied, lifting one hand to her heated cheek. "And we are very skilled at convincing fae to do what we want."

"Like make babies," she grumbled.

My lips twitched. "You want a faeling just as badly as the rest of us do. Don't let a little time shift convince you otherwise."

Her mouth parted to argue my choice of "little"— something I caught in her mental voice as she began to rage in her head again—so I silenced her with a gentle kiss, one that ended in her biting my bottom lip.

I soothed the ache away with my tongue before kissing her again and sliding my fingers back into her braid to hold her to me. There were so many things I could do with her hair in this state, all of them sexual in nature.

But I chose to merely embrace her, to allow her to feel my love and tranquility, to surround her with my inner element, and to allow it to soothe her inner turmoil.

We're in this together, I reminded her softly. *We all want the Interrealm Fae Academy to prosper. It will be a great place for our children to attend school. So trust us to help you, little queen. That's why we're here. The world doesn't always need to rest on your shoulders.*

She sighed, her arms slipping around my waist as she began to melt into my touch, her mind quieting.

I languidly deepened our kiss, drawing her into a state of contentment that I felt to my very soul. Exos stood, his heat blanketing her back as he clasped her hips before dropping his mouth to her neck.

She moaned between us, her smaller form surrounded by royalty and Elemental Fae power.

His palm slid between us, going to her lower belly, his mouth brushing her ear. "I can feel the faeling," he whispered to her. "I know you were worried earlier, Claire. I could sense it through the bond. But our future baby is healthy and growing, just as he or she should."

Our, she repeated in her mind, smiling. I grinned against her mouth, liking the sound of it, too. Because it didn't matter that I was the one who had fathered the child; all her mates would look at the faeling as *our* child.

"Let us take care of you," I said against her mouth. "That's why we're here."

"We'll handle the fae meetings," Exos added. "Just let us know what you want to be part of, and you'll be there. Otherwise, leave it with us. And focus on taking care of our faeling."

"It's not in my nature to just... give up control," she admitted, swallowing.

"Then tell us what to do," I offered. "Tell us what you need, and we'll help you achieve it. But don't carry all this around on your own, Claire. That's not going to work for any of us."

She nodded. "I know."

"Good." I kissed her nose, then pressed my forehead to hers. "Now I have another request."

Her eyebrow inched upward. "Another request?" She sounded cynical. "I think you've had enough requests."

I grinned. "This is one I think you'll like."

"Uh-huh."

I nibbled her lower lip, then pulled away just enough to look down at her blouse. "May we help you out of these wet clothes?"

She frowned, glancing down. "How…?" She blinked. "Hold on, what's the request? I'm not letting you use sex to distract me. Last time I did that, I ended up pregnant."

Rather than correct her statement, I merely said, "Stripping you is my request."

"Oh." She frowned, then looked down again. "Okay."

"While we're making requests," Exos added, his mouth against her throat again. "I would like to request fucking your ass."

Her cheeks flushed. "*Exos.*"

"And I want your pussy," I declared, enjoying how her skin darkened to a deep red shade. "Don't act like you're surprised by our bluntness, little queen. You've been mated to us long enough to know our preferences."

She swallowed. "I'm still not used to it."

My lips twitched again. "Then allow us to provide another demonstration." I started unfastening her blouse since she'd technically provided permission. "Consider this a practice round for phase three."

"And what happens in phase three?" she asked, breathless as we peeled the shirt from her gorgeous body.

"Intense sex," Exos whispered against her ear, his fist on her skirt, dragging it down her legs. "Now go get on the bed and spread those pretty thighs."

CLAIRE

OKAY, so there was a benefit to this whole pregnancy thing—*amazing sex*. And also, just my mates in general.

They had never been more attentive than they were now, which was saying a whole heck of a lot, considering they always seemed to bend over backward for me.

Such as now, with Titus helping me decorate the main meeting room of the chancellor building on campus. Cyrus had said to expect a few fae to drop by to discuss the Interrealm Fae Academy, and I'd gone into interior designer mode.

Holidays made people happy.

And I needed these fae to be happy.

Which was how I found myself in a sea of sequins, glitter, and festive winter décor. It covered every inch of the meeting chamber for today's guests. I just couldn't focus on the paperwork or potential negotiations, not until the room was properly prepared.

The term "nesting" repeated over and over again in my head, only driving me into a frenzy to make everything even more right.

But everywhere I turned, I found an empty space

that needed a Santa statue. A blank wall that was missing a splattering of glitter. A staircase in desperate need of more tinsel.

"Candles," I declared with a clap of my hands. Oh, yes, a sea of flickering lights would do the trick.

I needed my elements, even if I didn't have full access to them.

Yes, yes. Definitely candles.

Titus studied me as I used one of the already lit candles to carefully light the others one by one. He appeared ready to say something, when a stray puff of fake snow drifted through the room, nearly catching on fire. He arched the flame away from it with a sweep of his hand, his eyebrow inching upward at me.

"Thanks," I said shyly, hating that I was having to rely more and more on my mates to keep me from setting rooms on fire.

"Suddenly afraid of a little heat?" he asked with a sexy smile, planting a kiss on my lips. I indulged in the taste of him before I wriggled away to keep on with my work.

"I'm just being extra careful," I replied, meaning it.

"Yes, I can see that." He followed as I surveyed the room for the thousandth time.

The decorations seemed to take precedence over preparations for my impending meeting. However, Titus didn't point out my lopsided priorities.

Aflora and a few other fae would be walking through the door lined with holly any minute now. The rest of my mates would be joining as well to keep an eye on me. Cyrus in particular was protective as of late, understandably, and Titus was probably feeling the pressure to keep me safe as well.

"Do you really need to give me a heart attack

again?" Titus asked woefully, catching my side as I wobbled on a ladder. "Just tell me what needs to be hung up, and I'll do it. Or we could grab Vox."

"No," I replied, stubbornly taking each step up the ladder with Titus's hands firmly on my hips. "You wouldn't do it right." I was the only one who knew where everything had to go. Except I couldn't really explain that absurd sense of certainty to my mates.

Titus's warmth escalated out of frustration as I adjusted one of the snowflake streamers.

Usually, I would have used a little wind magic to cinch the tall loops into the ceiling, but my element wouldn't come to me.

That should have been concerning.

And yeah, I probably should have said something.

But the Healer had told me I might feel a little off my game as the faeling grew. And it wasn't like this Halfling pregnancy came with an instruction manual or anything.

So rather than fret over it, or unnecessarily worry my mates even further, I'd decided to stay calm and do what I could to make this feel more like a safe space.

Hence all the decorations.

A room full of festive cheer gave me the sense of calm I needed.

"Yes, there we are," I said, satisfied as I snagged the streamer swaying in between complementing layers of autumn leaves and pumpkins.

"Are you finally done?" he asked, his voice going up with a hopeful lilt.

"Hmm," I hummed, glancing around the room. Thanksgiving, Christmas, and Autumn and Winter Solstices all wrapped up the room in my festive masterpiece, but something was still missing.

"Um…" came an uncertain voice as Aflora inched the door open, pushing aside the faux snow I'd crammed too close to the hinges. A nearby candle flickered, and Titus twisted his fingers, sending the flame away before it lit the entire display on fire.

"Am I in the right place?" she asked, warily eyeing the candles.

"Aflora," I greeted, excited to see the female Sol referred to as his little sister. The two of them had grown up together after Aflora's Royal Fae parents died, and now the two of them shared access to the source of earth.

I waved my hands to beckon her to enter and immediately regretted the motion as I nearly fell off the ladder. Titus cursed and caught me, setting my feet on the ground.

Then a flame broke out across the room.

"Shit," Titus muttered.

Aflora pulled a wand from her cloak and muttered a spell, killing the fire with a few spare breaths. Then she looked around the room with her cerulean gaze.

"Well, there are enough decorations in here to decorate a field of wildflowers," she said. "Someone's definitely nesting."

Titus grunted in agreement as male voices cascaded through the open doorway. Zephyrus stepped through it while smirking at whatever Cyrus had just said.

"Wow, did Christmas and Thanksgiving have a baby?" Zephyrus asked, glancing around the room.

"Claire's nesting," Aflora replied.

"Yes, I see that," he deadpanned. "Hi, Claire." The greeting lacked affection, but that was standard from the Warrior Blood. Midnight Fae had a variety of classifications. His focused primarily on defensive magic, which echoed in his stance now as he went dutifully to Aflora's side. "Why is your wand out?"

"Fire," Aflora replied, putting the magical conduit away. "I'm fine."

He looked her over with pensive green eyes, his features sharp and cutting as he ensured she was truly "fine."

Cyrus arched a brow at me just as Titus jumped to take out a newly escaped flame.

"I thought nesting was supposed to help you make a *safe* space," my water mate teased, walking forward to brush his fingers under my chin. Mist washed over me, giving me a tingling sensation as he instinctively protected me with a shield of water.

I narrowed my eyes at him. "You don't need to put me in a literal bubble, Cyrus."

He smirked. "I do when you're intent on setting rooms on fire."

"I got this," Titus assured him, then hissed when another flame escaped his attention.

"You missed one, Firefly," Cyrus pointed out, earning a growl from my Fire Fae that promised vengeance.

I grinned, amused by their usual banter.

Gina poked her head through the door and glanced around the room, boasting a wry smile. "Did I miss the fireworks?"

"What fireworks—" I asked, only to be interrupted by an explosion that had me shrieking and clinging to Cyrus.

Aflora held a hand to her chest while Zephyrus narrowed his shrewd gaze. Titus's unruly flames— spurred on by Cyrus's "Firefly" taunt—had reached the appetizer trays of shelled nuts. Now they were exploding all over the ceiling. The life-sized nutcracker jostled next to the display, appropriately gyrating its mouth open and closed as it wobbled.

Gina clapped her hands, the only one among us who hadn't been surprised. Well, Zephyrus didn't look very surprised, so much as annoyed.

Cyrus doused the flames with a sweeping caress of his magic, careful not to soak my decorations in the process. However, he left the flames alight, likely to irritate Titus.

I can feel your amusement, baby, Exos murmured into my mind. *Causing chaos again?*

Just having fun with holiday decorations, I replied, my lips twitching.

Hmm, he hummed back, his own amusement reaching my heart. *I'll be there in a few minutes with Sol and Vox. I hope you're hungry.*

Why are we having so much food for a meeting? I wondered at him.

Maybe it's not for a meeting, he suggested.

What do you mean?

Patience, Claire.

If he were standing before me, I'd stick my tongue out at him in annoyance. Instead, Cyrus distracted me with his mouth by placing a kiss on my lips that left me sighing in contentment.

Aflora shuffled through the glitter to find a seat. She pushed aside some stuffed pillows in the shape of stars and Christmas trees before finally plopping down onto a chair. "I don't know where everybody else is going to sit." Zephyrus smirked and took the seat beside her.

I bit my lip as I studied the room, considering the problem. I'd just let my instincts fly and hadn't really considered logistics.

Gina swayed to a collection of faux snow and settled into it like a bird snuggling into a nest.

"I think this works just fine." She plucked at the puffy edges of her makeshift seat. "It reminds me of when my Omega instincts first took hold. It's a similar type of nesting instinct, I think." She gave me a smile, her eyes flashing with a hint of white as she grazed her fingers over the decorations that triggered one of her visions. "Welcome to pregnant life, Claire. It's going to keep you on the run."

"Claire?" came my name, paired with a worried feminine tone, before I had time to address Gina's strange statement. My mother walked in and halted, her eyes growing big. "Oh…"

"Oh, hi, Mom," I greeted, smiling. "We're having a meeting." Whenever all the other fae decided to arrive.

What time are they all coming, again? I asked Exos.

They're all arriving right now, he replied.

My eyes widened. *Oh, I'm not ready yet!*

You're fine, he replied. *Just talk to your mom.*

How do you know my mom is here?

No response.

"What is it, Ophelia?" Mortus asked as he entered after my mother, causing me to frown.

Why is Mortus here?

Because he's your mom's boyfriend, Exos replied.

Yeah, I know. But why is he attending the meeting?

Because we invited him, baby.

"What's my brother saying?" Cyrus asked softly, his arm circling my waist as he stepped to my side.

"I was asking him about the meeting," I muttered, then smiled as my mother and her boyfriend approached.

"Ah, yes. The 'meeting,'" Cyrus replied, an odd caress on that final word.

"Your mother warned me about your nesting, but you've really outdone yourself, Claire," Mortus said, leaning down to kiss my cheek. It was a bit strange seeing the former Fire Fae professor be so warm. He used to be such a dick. However, he hadn't exactly been himself then. "Happy nesting party," he added softly.

"Nesting party?" I repeated. "What?"

My mother playfully slapped him on the chest. "It was supposed to be a surprise, Mortus!"

"Oh. Right." He grimaced. "Sorry."

My mother sighed against him and just shook her head. "You're forgiven. Do you want to put the presents under the tree?"

He nodded. "Anything for you, sweetheart."

Their relationship had grown over the last few years, but they weren't really mated. I supposed he truly was more like my mother's boyfriend than a husband. Which was a really weird designation for him.

"What's a nesting party?" I asked, perking up at the idea of another festive occasion.

"*Fuck*," Titus cursed as another flame shot out of control.

Cyrus smirked. "Problems, Firefly?"

"Suck my cock," Titus snapped.

"Titus!" my mother gasped, making my fire mate flinch.

"Sorry, Ophelia," he said, sounding contrite.

Cyrus just grinned harder.

Stop taunting him, I said to my water mate.

But it's so fun, he replied.

I just shook my head and glanced at Gina, wondering if I should worry about more explosions, but her attention had diverted to the door as if she was waiting for more fae to enter.

Is a Hell Fae coming? I asked Exos.

Definitely not.

Shifter Fae? I guessed.

Nope, he replied.

Then who all is coming?

Patience, he repeated.

Sighing, I went back to the task of adjusting my decorations, which included ascending the ladder again to adjust another streamer.

"What are you doing up there?" my mother demanded, shock evident in her voice. "You shouldn't be tottering about at dangerous heights."

"Good luck convincing her to stop," Titus muttered, then cursed as fire raced up one of the curtains. "Damn it." He stilled the flame with a wave of magic.

"I don't like you up there," Cyrus said, his hands on my hips, steadying me while Titus focused on the candles. "Come down, please."

"I'm fine," I insisted. Vox and I often found ourselves in the clouds during one of our one-on-one sessions, but she didn't need to know that.

But I allowed him to pull me off the ladder anyway just as the rest of my mates entered.

Exos narrowed his gaze but didn't comment.

"Why aren't you steadying yourself with the earth?" Sol asked as he helped Vox place a mountain of food on the table near the burnt nuts. "And what happened here?"

"Claire likes candles," Titus explained.

"And she can handle heights just fine," Vox added, then frowned as glitter floated toward the food. He sent it away with a puff of air. "This stuff is everywhere."

"I know, and it's so pretty!" I exclaimed, lacking a better reason for why all of this was necessary.

He softened and smiled at me. "Yes, it's all beautiful. Just like you, Claire."

Exos smirked in amusement, then left for more food. When he returned, it was also with a bunch of plates and cutlery.

"Seriously, why do we need all this food for a meeting?" I asked him.

"Because it's not a meeting," he replied. "It's a surprise nesting party."

"Which isn't so much a surprise since everyone keeps telling her," Cyrus added dryly, his arm around my waist again.

"Okay, but what's a nesting party?" I asked again, hoping somebody would clarify. "And if it's not for the Interrealm Fae Academy, then I want an update on how all that is going."

Cyrus slipped behind me to wrap his arms around my waist, forcing me to face my mother. "Want to explain, Ophelia? This was all your idea, right?"

My mother giggled, the sound girlish for her age, as she sat down beside Mortus. Of course, she didn't look a day over thirty, and neither did her *boyfriend*. Fae genetics were kind of awesome like that.

"Yes, Cyrus is right. I'm to blame," she admitted as Mortus slid his arm around her. I wondered if they would ever decide to mate each other again. Their first mating hadn't been by choice. But they really did seem to love each other now.

"I wanted to surprise you with a nesting party, which is like a baby shower," she explained, making me recall Gina saying something like that to me last month. I met the Fortune Fae's gaze, and she gave me a dazzling smile. Right. She'd predicted this.

"So your mates helped me with this ruse," my mother continued. "You're in the heart of your nesting phase right now, so I thought you'd enjoy a little celebration." Her gaze swept across the room, then fell to my stomach, and her features softened into a smile. "Your little holiday heir will be here before we know it."

Holiday heir.

I liked the sound of that.

"So there's no meeting," I said. "But someone is going to update me on the Interrealm Fae Academy, right?" The only update I had was that they kept scheduling meetings all over the realms, providing information from my presentation and trying to secure alliances. There would be a big vote near the end of the year.

"How about after the nesting party?" Cyrus suggested, his lips against my ear. "Let's enjoy our faeling first, then Exos and I will shower you in political discussion."

My lips curved. "Promise?"

"We promise," he murmured, kissing my cheek.

I call your pussy this time, Exos said in my head, causing me to choke on my own tongue.

Exos!

What? He gave me a devious look from where he stood beside the food. *Do you prefer me in your ass?*

Stop. My mom is here. Right there. Staring at me.

And what a beautiful blush you're now wearing, he teased, winking at me from across the room.

I attempted to swallow, but Cyrus's warmth against my back made that difficult. Then Sol and Vox gave me heated stares from across the room as well, and it was like I'd become one of the unruly candles.

All of you need to stop, I said, blasting the message through the bonds.

I've not even started, Titus replied, his gaze reminding me of embers as he faced me.

"Nesting party time?" Cyrus offered softly. "What do you say, little queen?"

"Party time," I agreed.

"Not all presents are good for eating," Gina interjected, her commentary random and so completely like her.

I glanced back at Cyrus, who only shrugged in response.

"And the fun has arrived!" Lance announced as he swept into the room with his arms stretched wide and nearly knocking a candle to the ground. He righted it with the ease only a Fire Fae could possess.

"Lance," Titus hissed. "You're supposed to be visiting with Mum and Da right now, aren't you?"

"Mum and Da?" I repeated on a squeak. I hadn't seen Titus's family in years, and while they seemed to like me, Fire Fae ran a bit, uh, hot, to say the least. And Titus's relationship with his parents, as well as his brother, wasn't the best. He'd lost control of his powers when he was younger and had killed several extended family members in the process. Including Lance's favorite cousin.

"You didn't tell me your parents were here?"

"Because they're visiting my brother, not—"

A Fire Fae with gleaming red eyes and bulky muscles pushed into the room, halting Titus midsentence. His father paused to gape at the room, his heat causing the holly decorations around him to wilt. Sap dripped on his shoulder, making him frown. "Okay, we're here. Where's the food?"

"Pyros," his wife, Ruby, chided. She was a sweet little thing with bright red hair. For whatever reason, she always reminded me of cherries. "Say hello to your son's mate."

The Fire Fae cleared his throat. I had a feeling that my Fire-Fae-in-law—an adopted term I used for all the parents of my mates, even though it wasn't technically accurate—was not someone to be disobeyed. "Hi, Claire. Congratulations on the faeling."

That done, he made his way to the food and took his time filling one of the plates.

Titus came up beside me, and his lips brushed my ear. "Don't mind my da. He's just sour that a Water Fae got first dibs on an heir. It's yet another fault he'll lay at my doorstep."

Cyrus snorted, having overheard the comment.

Ruby approached, giving me a soft smile. "You look radiant, darling," she said as if in consolation to her husband's rudeness.

"Thank you, Ruby."

She patted my hand before taking a seat beside Gina. She moved on to making pleasant conversation, all the while not so subtly trying to encourage the Fortune Fae to tell her when she could expect a little Fire Faeling to appear.

Releasing a long breath, I allowed Cyrus and Titus to guide me to a chair. Then Sol handed me a plate he'd already prepared, and my mates crowded around me with dishes of their own.

It took me a little while to fully relax, but when nobody moved to dismember my decorations and instead found their way around them, I started to enjoy myself.

Vox fussed a little over the food as glitter continued to spoil his "perfect creations." However, Sol insisted it added a crunch that had been missing, much to Vox's detriment. My Earth Fae mate really loved all food, regardless of the origin or type.

Cyrus and Exos also caved and gave me the updates I wanted regarding the academy. They were all positive, save the Hell Fae issue.

"We might need to consider moving forward without them," Cyrus said.

I shook my head. "We need them."

"They've not been part of fae society for centuries, Claire," Exos murmured.

"And I want to fix that," I insisted. "Think about it. If an Interrealm Fae Academy had existed before, this never wou—"

"Would have been an issue," Exos and Cyrus finished for me.

My water mate blew out a breath and shook his head. "I promise to keep trying."

"That's all I ask," I replied.

"I know." He cupped my cheek and bent to brush a kiss over my lips.

"So where did you train?" Lance's voice carried across the room. He'd chosen to sit next to Zephyrus— something that clearly made the Midnight Fae uncomfortable. Aflora seemed to find it amusing, though.

When Zephyrus didn't respond, Lance added, "I've held the Powerless Champion title for the past three years."

Still no reply, but I suspected the Warrior Blood was

talking to Aflora mentally, because her eyes were sparkling with unrestrained laughter.

"Do the Midnight Fae have any fighting rings?" Lance pressed.

The Warrior Blood narrowed his eyes, giving a succinct answer. "None where an Elemental Fae would be welcome."

Lance puffed his chest up, taking that for the challenge it was. I bit my lip, wondering if I should intervene before the hotheaded Fire Fae had his ass handed to him.

When I was about to get up, Titus pushed a present under my nose that smelled of... a sort of cinnamon?

My stomach pitched.

Normally, I liked cinnamon, even the fae variety, but I wasn't sure I could handle more fae food right now. My stomach was already rolling from the food my mates had put on my plate, and I'd barely touched it.

So, yeah, trying something new did not appeal to me right now.

"It's from my family," he explained, obviously proud of the gift. "You did remember to pack it correctly, right?" he asked Lance pointedly.

His brother rolled his eyes. While his muscular build reminded me of Titus, he had a harsher edge to him, taking after their father more, whereas Titus more closely resembled their mother. "It's exactly as you instructed," the younger Fire Fae assured him before turning back to a still-uninterested Zephyrus.

Titus gave the package a light shake, then planted it in my lap. "Open it," he encouraged me, keeping his lips close to the curve of my neck as he brushed my hair aside.

I smiled and undid the tie, then unwrapped the shiny

red foil to reveal an adorable little cinnamon cake etched with glowing embers.

"Will it burn me if I try to eat it?" I asked, my stomach churning. I really hoped this didn't make me sick.

How humiliating would it be to vomit at my own nesting party? *Ugh.*

I loved when Titus surprised me with new fae treats, but this couldn't have been worse timing.

Titus brought the treat to my mouth and swayed it under my nose, causing my insides to churn in protest.

Yeah, this wasn't going to work.

"It's a fire cake," he explained, oblivious to my agony. "I think our little faeling will love…"

Just when I felt like the contents of my stomach were about to come up, the cake erupted into a massive flame, making everyone shriek.

Shit. Did I do that?

I most certainly hadn't cast any magic, but the fire element that burned the gift to a crisp—literally—had come from me.

Or… from *within* me.

Pyros barked out a laugh. "Now that's a fire cake. Nice."

"But I didn't—" I protested while Titus stormed over to his father.

"Do you think this is some sort of joke?" Titus boomed. "Why are you here if you're going to ruin everything?"

Titus's father puffed out his chest. "I didn't burn your cake, if that's what you're implying." He landed a hand on Lance's shoulder, making the fae flinch. "Although, it was pretty funny, wouldn't you say, Lance?"

The younger Fire Fae did not appear to be laughing

at all, nor did he seem amused by his father's hand on his shoulder.

"I'm afraid it's my fault," Cyrus interjected. "I rather detest fire cakes. It's a Water Fae thing. Maybe Claire is taking on some of my preferences during the pregnancy?"

Titus frowned, but the suggestion wasn't enough to cool him off.

Gina held up a package she'd plucked from under the tree. "Oh, look, a present from Sol's family!" she announced. She hurried to me and brushed away the drifting ash before dropping the gift onto my lap. She leaned down and whispered, "A distraction will keep the Fire Fae from blowing up."

Titus grumbled but returned to my side as I unwrapped the item. The decorative tissue held a large green leaf. I held it up to the light. "Do I, uh, eat this, too?" I asked, afraid it might erupt into flames like the last edible item did.

Sol chuckled. "It's a swaddle, little flower."

I turned it over and raised an eyebrow. "Oh… um, thanks?" I said, giving him a weak smile before putting the leaf back into the tissue paper.

The gift-giving continued as the fae offered me more presents—some of which I hadn't even noticed beneath the tree, thanks to magical enchantments crafted by Aflora and the others.

Each present was stranger than the last.

Gina gave me a row of sticks that supposedly would help me predict nap times.

Aflora and Zephyrus gifted me with a seed that they stated I would not want to plant. Something about burning thwomps and only using it as a protective measure.

Vox's family had sent a rather annoying set of wind chimes that I suspected had a curse attached to it.

My mother and Mortus provided the most normal present of them all—a book of elemental stories to read to our faeling when she or he was older.

I started to read it as a distinct sensation made me cross my legs and start to squirm. *Crap.*

"What is it?" Cyrus asked, placing a hand on my knee.

Sol wrapped his fingers around the curve of my shoulder in that possessive way I liked. He had sensed my sudden discomfort, too. I almost allowed it to lull me into a state of comfort.

Until my bladder protested and forced me into action.

I shot up, flinging my mates off of me. "Bathroom!" I shouted, not caring how everyone openly stared at me as a sudden, inexplicable urge swept through my body. "Gotta... pee!"

Gina's prophetic words followed me as I bolted out of the room.

Welcome to pregnant life, Claire. It's going to keep you on the run.

CLAIRE

CYRUS STOOD outside of the bathroom, waiting for me.

"Ready for another gift?" he asked, a hint of promise in his voice.

"Is it sex?" I guessed.

His lips quirked upward at the sides. "That's a given, not a gift," he drawled, holding out his arm for me. "Come on, Exos and I want to show you something. And no, that's not a euphemism."

"With you two, it's hard to know for sure," I muttered.

"Definitely hard," Exos echoed.

The two males laughed, and I just shook my head. "I rest my case."

Cyrus wrapped his arm around me, steering me away from the nesting party and toward the building's exit. "Where are we going?" I asked.

"Home," he replied.

"Without saying bye to everyone?" I asked, frowning.

"I'll mist you back for that," he promised as Exos took my hand and walked along on my other side.

"All right. I'm holding you to that." Not that I really wanted to return to the party, but it seemed rude to leave without at least expressing my gratitude to everyone.

Especially Aflora and Gina, who had traveled the realms to get here.

Titus, Vox, and Sol joined us outside, their gazes all filled with questions.

"You don't know what their gift is, do you?" I asked them.

A chorus of negatives met my question.

Which meant this was all Exos and Cyrus. Great. "Nothing good happens when you two are working together," I grumbled, not really meaning it. But I wanted to know what they had planned for me.

"Nothing at all?" Cyrus replied, his hand slipping lower onto my backside. "You seem to enjoy it when Exos and I work together."

I shivered, Exos's comments from earlier warming my mind. "Well, maybe there are exceptions."

Titus grunted.

"Jealous, Firefly?" Cyrus taunted him.

"Fuck off, Jackass," Titus retorted.

"That's *Royal* Jackass to you," Cyrus corrected.

My fire mate just shook his head, his demeanor displaying his exhaustion. He'd worked hard keeping all those flames under control today. Because I hadn't been able to help.

My lips twisted. I really needed to say something, but how did I bring it up? Like, *Oh, by the way, I can't access the elements. Okay. Good chat.*

They were all being so protective already. That would just make it worse.

Except, my not talking to them also caused problems. I really should—

"Cyrus has been bragging about his present to you all week," Titus murmured, distracting me. "But he wouldn't tell us what it is." He glowered at the Water

King. "I *had* been hoping to overshadow him with a fire cake, but that blew up in my face."

Vox chuckled. "Literally." He patted the Fire Fae on the arm as we started up the path to our home. It wasn't too far from the Chancellor's office—since I was the Chancellor. But we had built the two buildings separately, unlike my predecessor, who lived and worked in the same place.

"We can make one together," Vox added, taking pity on my fire mate. "I'd love to learn the recipe."

Titus opened the door to our house. "There was a reason I had my brother bring the present. It's a highly guarded secret through my mum's line. Good luck getting it out of her."

"Challenge accepted," Vox said, his eyes gleaming as he stepped through the threshold. My air mate seemed determined to learn all cuisine secrets, human, fae, or otherwise.

My stomach rumbled, reminding me that I hadn't been able to enjoy any of his typically scrumptious meals for a few days now. I hoped whatever Cyrus and Exos planned to surprise me with came with a side of hamburgers and fries.

Cyrus undid his tie as we entered our home and stepped in front of me. I lifted my brow. "And what do you plan to do with that?" I asked.

"Blindfold you." He wrapped the soft silk over my eyes, and Exos released my hand to step behind me and helped his brother tie the strands against my hair.

"You said this wasn't about sex," I reminded him. "Not that I'm complaining."

He chuckled. "I just want to make sure you get the full effect," he promised. Although, the tug in our mate-bonds suggested he wouldn't mind a little foreplay follow-up later.

Exos took my hand again. I knew it was him because his kiss of spirit magic always called to my heart. It made me miss my elements even more.

However, my mates' magic seemed to surge through me more and more lately, as though providing me with much-needed nourishment directly from the elemental source.

It felt odd to describe it that way.

Their magic had never given me that sensation before, but their touch somehow eased my hunger, so I clung to Exos, drawing out the tingling strand between us as we walked.

My mates guided me through our home and toward the secondary bedroom we had set up for guests or visiting family members.

Not that we really ever entertained any.

Our nightly activities made it kind of difficult. And my mom lived just off campus with Mortus, so she didn't ever have a reason to stay.

Hmm, in retrospect, with the bedroom just two doors down from ours, it was a poor choice for guest quarters. But it was one of the bigger rooms, so it had once made sense to use it for guests.

Except, now I suspected my mates had a different purpose in mind, which caused my heart to flutter at the *gift* Cyrus and Exos had intended for me. I tried not to get my hopes up, telling myself this probably wasn't at all what I thought, but the subtle kiss of water in the air—a kiss that hadn't been there this morning—had all my instincts firing to life.

Someone opened the door, and approval surged through my mate-bonds, making me even more anxious to see. "Can I take off my blindfold?" I asked, my nostrils flaring at the alluring scent of mist and a calming fragrance that reminded me of the spirit realm.

"Not yet," Cyrus said, water warming my bare arms, making the hairs stand on end as if electrified. He guided me another step forward, then whispered, "Okay, now."

I jerked off the silk tie and gasped at the sight before me.

"Oh, Fae," I said, taking in the enchanted nursery scene swarming with water and spirit magic.

A purple butterfly kissed my cheek, causing my eyes to wander sideways to Exos. He grinned, then gestured to the array of beautiful spirit-infused creatures fluttering about. No pixies, just butterflies. My favorite.

A fountain resided in the corner, the gorgeous structure pumping moisture and magic into the room with a small basin beside it that would be good for bathing a newborn. I moved forward to brush my fingers through the warm spray, smiling at the sense of calm provided by the source itself.

Beyond the fountain was a window providing a breathtaking view of Sol's white Christmas trees.

But the most elaborate piece rested against the wall.

I stepped up to the ornate crib with glowing blue spirals. I touched it, expecting to find glass, but my fingers grazed a warm, smooth texture that slightly gave way underneath my touch. It was unlike any material I'd ever seen.

"It's a magical water construct that's safe for teething," Cyrus explained, his hand going to the small of my back. "I had intended on buying human furniture, but when my father's mate showed me what the royal line had access to, combined with our own enhancement magic, well, I knew you'd love it."

"I do," I said, running my fingers over the gorgeous work of art. I chewed my lip as one hand went to my belly. Cyrus's touch followed, his embrace warming me to my core.

"Hmm, but I think it's missing something," Exos said, stroking his jaw as he considered the room. "I think we need some earth."

Sol studied the room, then rubbed his hands together before going to work on a cherry blossom tree in the corner opposite the fountain, adding a burst of pink to the overly blue room.

I inhaled the scent, my heart fluttering in response.

"And maybe some fire," Exos added.

"On it," Titus said, adding delicate embers that floated to the ceiling, capturing warmth like tiny little stars.

"And air," Cyrus murmured, glancing at Vox.

The Air Fae grinned, his essence whirling upward to bring the whole scene together with a calming song humming on the wind, the ancient melody one that had my eyes drooping in sudden tiredness.

It's a faeling nursery rhyme, he explained into my mind. *It'll calm our little one.*

It's calming me right now, I admitted.

Good, he replied. *That means it's working.*

"This is... the most enchanting nursery I've ever seen," I whispered, relaxing into Cyrus. "Thank you."

My water mate lifted me with ease into his arms, my head pillowing against his shoulder. "Thank you, Claire," he replied, kissing my temple. "You're doing all the hard work. We're just trying to help where we can."

I wasn't so sure about that.

This didn't feel all that hard.

In fact, it sort of felt like a dream. One I never wanted to wake from. So I closed my eyes and allowed it to overtake me.

I love you all, I said softly into their minds, yawning. *I'll show you just how much when I wake up.*

VOX

A WEEK LATER

THERE WERE ingredients all over the damn kitchen.

I'd taken every single item out of the cupboards and shelves to see what I could possibly make for my mate that wouldn't result in her losing her meal after five minutes—or, in last night's case, before she'd even had a chance to ingest it.

"Maybe I should try a different type of peach tree," Sol suggested as he rubbed the back of his neck. He was just as frustrated as I was about Claire's latest pregnancy symptom.

We were in charge of Claire's well-being while Titus dealt with his family and Cyrus went with Exos to make final arrangements for today's meeting with the Hell Fae —something none of us were very keen about, especially now.

All the more reason for Claire to be nourished and at her best. And I had about an hour to make that happen.

I held up the remaining bag of grains I'd used to make porridge, something painfully simple and bland, but maybe she'd be able to keep it down. The bowl steamed on the counter, cooling while we waited for

Claire to awaken. I hated to give my mate something so tasteless, but nothing else had worked yet, and I was determined to give her body something to keep up with her—literal—growing demands.

"Ugh. This isn't going to work," I said, slamming the package down. The bag burst open as my magic spiraled out of control—*again*—sending food and packages tumbling over the counter from a powerful gust of wind.

Sol frowned as a lump of troll fat tumbled onto the floor. "Maybe we should make a new dish and tell her it's a popular human food? That worked last time, right?" he asked as he stomped over to the rubbery substance, the ground trembling in his wake. He plucked the fat from the floor and placed it back onto the counter with a mild smile. "She still eats it when we call it bacon."

I rolled my eyes. "She's not going to fall for that again." A whimper caught on the wind swirling through the hall, telling me Claire was awake again. I straightened and grabbed the bowl of porridge. "You woke her up with your stomping around."

Sol followed me—still stomping—as I briskly walked with a lighter stride to the master bedroom. "Yeah, I'm sure the crash of food all over our kitchen had nothing to do with it," he muttered back at me.

"What are you guys arguing about?" Claire moaned as she shifted within the bedsheets.

Fae, she was gorgeous, even more so now with that alluring curve to her belly. Her nightgown clung to her as she moved, revealing plump breasts with nipples hardening against the chill wind I'd brought into the room. I immediately found the warmer currents from higher in the rafters and began to bring them down.

Seeing Claire like this made my stomach do flips. The child would be born in roughly four or five weeks, and soon she would struggle to keep up with the accelerated growth of the faeling inside of her.

"Not too fast," I warned her when she slipped her foot over the bedside and tried to stand. She stumbled, her sense of balance seeming to fail her—likely from lack of food.

She grabbed onto me.

"Oh," she said, smiling when I caught her with ease, using a kiss of wind to wrap warm currents around her body so she wouldn't be cold. Goose bumps sprinkled over her arms before she sighed into the embrace of my magic.

Sol took her elbow, steadying her until she waved us off, determined to stand on her own two feet. "Stop fussing. I can walk just fine."

I narrowed my eyes at her as she swayed again.

"You need to keep up your strength," I said. Her once flushed cheeks were now sunken in. Her golden locks had flattened after too much time rolling over her pillow, and when she turned, I spotted hints of her rib cage as her gown clung to her back. Her arms and legs had lost their lean tone, and I wasn't the only one worried that she wasn't getting the nutrition she needed.

I held up my latest effort—porridge. "Can you eat?"

She eyed the dish warily. "No spices?" she asked.

"None."

She glanced at Sol. "No fruit… or fat?"

He smirked. "Neither fruit nor fat," he confirmed.

She took the bowl and sat on the edge of the bed, staring into it. "I feel like I have a bowling ball in my stomach," she muttered.

I smiled even though I had no idea what a bowling ball was. "Here," I said, taking the spoon and offering her a bite. "Give it a try."

She gently blew on it, although that wasn't necessary. I used tendrils of air to run over the offering to make sure it was the perfect temperature before it reached her lips. She took the spoonful, tried to swallow, then clamped a hand over her mouth before making a strangled sound.

I snatched up the bowl before she flung it onto the floor, and she ran to the bathroom.

Sighing, I handed my failed attempt at a meal to Sol. "Could you get rid of this, please? And add porridge to the list of foods she can't eat."

Sol cocked a brow. "I think we'd have a shorter list of things she *can* eat."

"When I find something, I'll start one," I replied flatly as I followed Claire and tried to think of something else she could stomach.

CLAIRE

"Where are you?" Titus called, his voice drifting into the bedroom.

I leaned against Vox for support while I held a washcloth to my mouth. I didn't like my mates seeing me in this state, but each of them had proved that they were going to be there for me through all of it.

If the last few days hadn't run them off, then I was pretty sure nothing would.

"We're in here," Vox replied, his words carrying on the wind as he brushed hair from my sweat-dampened face. "Do you feel any better?" he asked, lowering his voice. His fingers continued to stroke my temple in calming circles, easing my constant sense of nausea.

"Some," I said, although I definitely didn't feel my best. Hunger constantly gnawed at me, but I couldn't stomach any of this fae food. I didn't want to admit to my guys that it might be a cultural thing. I'd lived here for years, but my instincts craved food from home, like caramel-coated popcorn and salted meats. My mouth watered just thinking of it, and Vox misunderstood the groan that came from my mouth.

"What hurts?" he asked, running his hands over me. "Should I fetch the Healer?"

I grabbed his hands and kissed his fingertips. "Vox, I'm fine. I'm just hungry, but I'll survive."

Titus poked his head into the bathroom. "Hey, nobody invited me to the bathroom party." His eyes swept over my body, taking in my thin gown that did little to hide my curves or my breasts. His gaze lingered on the latter, appreciating how my nipples protested against the cool breeze he'd let into the warm room.

"I thought you were busy with Lance," Vox said, his voice holding a note of irritation. Although, I had a feeling he was just angry at himself for failing to find me something to eat.

"He's showing our parents the Fire Quad and his newly amassed row of Powerless Champion trophies," Titus said, poorly hiding his displeasure at his younger brother's success. The two of them were always at odds. It didn't help that their parents clearly favored Lance and frequently commented on his ability to control his powers, thereby alluding to the one time Titus hadn't.

Anyone else would have been miserable over the constant reminders of his failures.

But not Titus.

He had accepted his past a long time ago—before we'd even met—and lived his life the way he wanted to, without a care in the world as to what his parents thought of him.

I loved him for it. I also understood it because I, too, had once hurt those I cared about through an unexpected blast of power.

Titus slipped into the room and wrapped his arms around my torso, running his fingers over my enlarged belly, choosing to focus on me instead of his family quarrels. "How are you feeling today, Claire?"

"She's weakened," Vox snapped, not giving me a

chance to respond. "If you're done prancing around campus, why don't you help me find her something to eat?"

"Don't fight," I sighed, glaring at him as I untangled myself from their wandering hands. "I'm just going to take a nap."

"A nap?" Titus repeated. "You can't take a nap."

"Why not?" I asked, my brow furrowing.

They both stared at me for a moment. "You don't remember?" Titus finally questioned.

"The meeting you had scheduled with the Hell Fae before the final vote?" Vox supplied when I blinked up at both of them, confused.

I tilted my head. "Meeting? That wasn't until the end of the week, right?"

Titus and Vox shared a look before my Fire Fae replied, his words patient and slow. "It *is* the end of the week, Claire."

What?!

Cursing, I jerked open one of the drawers and pulled out a hairbrush, then ripped it through my strands. As if the physical state of my pregnancy wasn't bad enough, these damn memory gaps were going to be the death of me. "Well, that's okay. I'll just get myself together and..." I trailed off, searching for my toothbrush. Definitely going to need that.

"Are you sure you're up for this?" Vox asked, his tone concerned. "We could reschedule."

"Nope." I yanked the hairbrush through an unruly patch of my hair, then tossed it onto the counter and started brushing my teeth.

Both of my mates watched me with unease, waiting for me to finish my rapid brushing.

"Cyrus has been working to bring me a Hell Fae

representative for weeks," I said after spitting out some of my toothpaste. "By the time we could meet with someone new, I'll have a baby to deal with."

And then that would take all my priority.

After the faeling came, the last thing I would be able to focus on would be forcing fae to work together. No, I couldn't leave this job half-done before I became a mother.

Plus, what kind of world would I be bringing my baby into if I didn't have the groundwork established for a place like the Interrealm Fae Academy? A place where my child would eventually be welcomed.

Not an abomination.

But a blessing.

Titus crossed his arms. "I still don't like this, Claire. Hell Fae are fickle creatures at the best of times, and, well, just plain *hell* when they're unhappy. They're not going to want to work with us. Not after what the fae did to them."

Ignoring him, I splashed cold water on my face. "They're just misunderstood. I'm going to fix that." It was one of the many reasons I wanted the Interrealm Fae Academy to exist—so none of fae kind experienced the torments the Hell Fae and other abominations had endured.

Once I'd dried my skin, Vox held up a concealer stick that Cyrus had picked up during one of his Human Realm trips, at my request. I liberally applied it to the dark spots under my eyes.

Vox said nothing while Titus leaned against the wall and watched as I tried to hide the evidence of my exhaustion.

"One false move and I'm burning them all," he said, his tone lacking his trademark humor.

LEXI C. FOSS & J.R. THORN

"Yeah, burn the Hell Fae. That's a brilliant idea," Vox deadpanned. "Not like they haven't dealt with fire before."

Titus frowned. "Then Cyrus will blast them into the ocean and drown them under leagues of water. I don't care how it happens. If they mess with Claire, they're dead. That's all I'm saying."

Vox tied his loose strands into his favored warrior's tail as if preparing for a fight. "Agreed."

With a sigh, I decided it would be a Christmas miracle if this meeting went even remotely as planned.

Speaking of Christmas...

"Hey, Titus?" I asked, going onto my tiptoes to lean into the mirror and apply my blush. If I got much bigger, I'd have to pick up my stomach to do this. "Do Hell Fae like Christmas presents?"

TITUS DIDN'T THINK it was a good idea, but really, who didn't like presents?

I marched toward my office with my gift in hand, meticulously packaged with my best silver wrapping paper topped with a glimmering bow. Thanks to Titus, twinkling embers studded the exterior, giving it a smoldering look that I thought a Hell Fae might appreciate.

It felt good to step into my office, which Sol and Vox had perfectly redecorated. Gone were the autumn decorations of October, and in their place was a gorgeous white Christmas tree. It sprouted from the center of the room, a living creation courtesy of my earth mate. Glimmering stars and sparkles danced on a rotation around the ceiling as well, the current a loop created by Vox's affinity for air.

I sighed in contentment. Because it really did feel like true Christmas magic.

However, one thing did not go with the festive, wintry decor, and that was the Hell Fae sitting in my chair with her legs propped up on the desk.

Cyrus shrugged when I came in. "It was the only way I could keep her waiting."

"That's all right," I said, smiling. I'd erase the scorch marks from my chair later. I had a Fire Fae for a mate. Flames often happened around upholstery.

My mates all insisted on joining the meeting with the Hell Fae representative and surrounded me like a protective barrier. She didn't look so terrifying, though. She had a warmth about her that reminded me of a Fire Fae, but that was where the similarities ended.

Horns protruded from glossy, midnight hair, and a disturbing growl rumbled in her chest as she swung her high-heeled knee-high boots off my desk. She glared up at me with eyes that glowed with ember red that had a sinister look to them as she tapped her manicured fingers across the wood.

"You're late," she stated, her tone flat with a hint of annoyance. However, I suspected my tardiness wasn't the only thing that agitated her.

I put on my best smile and placed the gift on the desk. I held out a hand. "It's such a pleasure to meet you. I'm Claire. And your name is?"

She stared at my hand for a moment, tapped her fingers on the desk again, and then pushed aside the gift she clearly didn't care about. Her gaze dropped to my protruding stomach that stuck out between the layers of my council robes. "What is *that?*" she asked, lifting her lip into a sneer.

"*That* is our child," Cyrus said with an edge of warning to his tone. Water droplets formed in the air, a warning of his power. "You'd be wise to be respectful in our realm."

Red streaks of molten power ran over her arms and writhed across her skin like a living entity in response to the threat. She rolled her eyes, kicked away from my desk, and stood on her high-heeled boots.

"And you'd be wise not to bring me out of my realm for this bullshit. I thought you said I was going to meet your queen of the five sources. I only came up here because Lucifer is intrigued by her naivety." She crossed her arms and glowered. "So instead of trying to bore me with pleasantries, how about we get to the point and—"

A flare of heat made us all jump. I'd been so focused on the Hell Fae that I hadn't noticed her brush against the Christmas tree. Hellfire spread throughout the delicate branches, igniting it like a matchstick. It roared with flames. Titus attempted to stop it, but his element didn't work against the foreign fire.

"Cyrus!" he shouted, shoving me out of harm's way. "Do something!"

Sparks of magic electrified at my fingertips, and a sharp kick hit me from inside. I gasped, realizing that I'd just felt my faeling for the first time, not because of excitement, but because of distress.

Cyrus doused the tree with a wave of water, leaving steam to fog the room as the stench of burned evergreen tinged my nose. Tears welled in my eyes when I saw my beautiful tree burned to a crisp. Hellfire didn't hold back.

Sol immediately went to my side. "Don't cry, little flower."

He stroked my head with broad, sweeping movements as my cries morphed into sobs. It didn't make sense that I'd get so upset about a burned tree, but it felt like a metaphor for my life.

No matter how hard I tried, everything just went up in flames.

It had always been that way for me. My first experience with fae magic had resulted in me burning down a bar with my friends still inside. Was this going to be what motherhood was like? Would I just be terrible at anything I tried to do? Would more people die because I couldn't get my shit together?

The self-doubt only made me sob harder, and I couldn't explain it to my mates, who were all trying to control the situation.

Sol shoved me into Cyrus's grip. "Fix this," he demanded while he went to the tree and worked an excessive show of magic, forcing the branches to warp and change as he brought it back to life.

Vox helped him, brushing away the ash into the cracks in the ground as the revived tree took shape. Exos grabbed the Hell Fae's arm and pulled her aside before she could burn anything else. She hissed at him, which would have been comical had I not been holding on to Cyrus like a hysterical loon crying over a tree Sol was already reviving.

It's okay, little queen. He's fixing it. He brushed his lips against my temple. *Shh, it's okay.*

His words only made me cry more.

Then Sol finished, and the tree was fuller, larger, and even more beautiful than before. The unique, white-feathered branches brushed the ceiling as Vox sent glitter and sparkles to dance around it. Titus snapped his fingers, creating a delicate blue glow to illuminate the top.

And my sobs increased.

It was just so sweet, and all of it was so, so beautiful. My mates would do anything to make me happy, even if it was something frivolous like fixing a Christmas tree.

And oh, I didn't deserve them.

Or any of this.

I couldn't even eat porridge right!

The Hell Fae gawked at me before glancing questioningly at Exos. I saw him mouth, "Pregnancy hormones," before she smirked.

I should have been mad, but I didn't care. I knew I was being unreasonably emotional. But what did they expect? I was growing a faeling in nine *weeks*. Not months. *Weeks*.

"Why are you still crying, little flower?" Sol asked, coming back to brush the tears from my face while I clung to Cyrus like a lifeline.

"It's just so *beautiful*," I said, smiling now as the tears continued to come, but this time they were tears of happiness. "Thank you." Then I looked at Cyrus. "Nine *weeks*. How did you expect me to do this in *nine weeks?*"

He blinked. "Claire…"

"No, this is your fault!" I pointed to my belly, then melted as the little faeling kicked again. "Oh my Fae, it's so cute. Did you feel that?"

"I did," Cyrus replied, his palm against my stomach and his lips curling. "Do it again," he encouraged, a note of wonder in his voice.

I relaxed into him, content.

Then the Hell Fae gagged, ruining the moment. "Seriously, this is why our kind have our Hellhounds raise the faelings to toughen them up. Who has time for this shit?"

Cyrus narrowed his eyes. "If you're done upsetting our mate, we brought you here to discuss the Interrealm Fae Academy plans. You're a proxy for Lucifer's vote, correct?"

She rolled her eyes. "Yeah, but no. I'm not interested. If he wants to work with you lunatics, he can come up here and vote for himself." She stormed out of the room. Vox followed her movements with a gust of wind to keep her hellfire from burning any of the festive decorations again.

Exos sighed. "I'll go after her."

Cyrus reluctantly guided me into his brother's arms. "No, it was my job to obtain the Hell Fae vote, and I messed it up. I'll fix it." He rested his hand on my stomach, smiling when the faeling kicked again. "You're doing a great job, Claire. Don't cry, and don't stress. I'll make sure the Hell Fae support the project."

Sniffling, I nodded. Cyrus gave me a quick kiss before he followed the smell of burned Christmas tree out of the room.

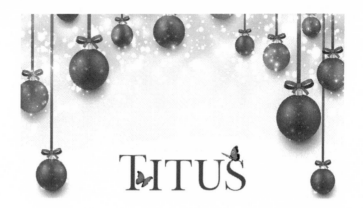

TITUS

"SOMETHING'S NOT RIGHT." I kept my voice low, not wanting to wake Claire in the other room. Sol had stayed in there with her because he was the loudest of all of us. Which meant we would hear them coming if she decided to wake up.

He knew what we planned to discuss out here.

It was weighing on all our minds—Claire's refusal to eat and her odd relationship with the elements.

"When was the last time someone saw her use an element?" Exos asked, his arms folded across his broad chest.

We'd all agreed that her reactions in her office with the Hell Fae were all wrong. She'd reacted like a helpless faeling, not a queen. And while we could grant her some leeway because she was pregnant and didn't want to put the child at risk, we also all felt the disconnect in her inaction.

What happened to our fae who had taken on a dangerous abomination via the spirit realm? A Hell Fae shouldn't frighten her. I mean, sure, they were terrifying as fuck, but the one in her office had barely lifted a finger, and Claire had wilted like some sort of weeping flower.

Exos thought it was hormones.

Maybe he was right.

But that didn't explain the other events or how she couldn't seem to eat anything we gave her.

"It's been a while," Vox said slowly. "Around the time of the consummation."

I nodded. "I've spent the most time with her lately while you all have been handling other things. And she's not used her elements at all. Not even to dry her hair."

"That could be her Water Fae coming out a little," Cyrus said, sounding thoughtful, not arrogant. "Most of my kind prefer wet hair for obvious reasons."

"Okay." I could give him that. "But she's been avoiding fire. She claims it's for safety reasons, but since when has she feared flames?"

"She's also not been using air at all to stabilize herself when on ladders," Vox added.

"She shouldn't be on any ladders," Cyrus reminded him, his annoyance palpable.

"Yes, yes," Exos replied, waving him off. "But the more important point is that she's not using her elements."

"Or eating," Vox muttered. "I tried to give her porridge today, and she couldn't even accept that." He palmed the back of his neck and blew out a breath. "Sol suggested we fake human food, but I'm thinking we should try real human food. We've already missed that Thanks Day holiday since it was this week. I couldn't find a bird, or whatever it was we needed, and River said I had waited too long for him to gather the ingredients. Besides, I wasn't even sure she would eat it."

"A turkey," Exos corrected. "Which is a type of bird, but Thanksgiving—which is the holiday's name—is all about the turkey. And we probably should have made her one."

"Maybe we need to take her home," Cyrus interjected. "For Christmas."

My brow furrowed. "Um, she's already home." Unless he meant the Water Kingdom? "Is she eating at the palace?"

"No, not an elemental home," he replied. "*Her* home. As in the Human Realm."

"Ohio," Exos murmured, his expression pensive. "It would take some time to organize, but that might be what she needs. While her fae side is dominant, she is still half-human."

"Can you put it together?" Cyrus asked.

Exos nodded. "Yeah, most of the fae on my list have already agreed to the academy. The only real outstanding kingdom is the Hell Fae."

Cyrus groaned. "Don't remind me. Those fuckers are going to be the death of me."

"Do we really need them to agree?" Vox asked, sounding wary.

"In theory, no," Exos replied. "But Claire really wants them involved. You know how she feels about making them feel welcome."

Yeah, we all did. She was under the misguided notion that the Hell Fae needed to be involved to try to reconcile the past. Since they were a kingdom of abominations, they were exactly the kind of mixed fae she was trying to help through this initiative.

The thing she failed to realize was that the Hell Fae were beyond help. They'd developed their own manner of existing centuries ago, and no amount of groveling now would turn back time. Even with a Paradox Fae's help.

I blew out a breath. "Right. So we'll plan a trip to the Human Realm. Is that where we want to be for phase three?"

Cyrus glanced at Exos. "We're going to need a big bed if we do that."

"It worked in Iceland," he pointed out. "I'm sure I can figure something out in Ohio."

"We'll need space, too," Vox warned. "She's connected to all five elements. We have no idea what that's going to do when she falls into the final phase."

"She should mostly take from water since the child is tied to our shared element," Cyrus said. "But I'm also half Spirit Fae. And as you said, she has all five elements."

"Assuming she even has access to them," I muttered.

"If she doesn't, she will," Exos replied. "It's not uncommon for the faeling to absorb from the source while in the womb. However, she's not said anything about it."

"You know Claire. She wants to do it all herself." And it drove me flipping nuts. "We need to keep an eye on her."

Exos smirked. "Like we haven't been doing that already."

"You know what I mean," I muttered, dragging my fingers through my auburn hair. It was sticking up on all ends today, thanks to that Hell Fae meeting. Fucking hellfire bitch. What was she thinking lighting the Christmas tree on fire? Ugh.

"Yeah, I do," Cyrus said softly. "We need to be extra guarded. If she can't access her elements, then she can't properly protect herself."

"Will that be a problem in the Human Realm?" Vox

asked. "Taking her somewhere new when she can't protect herself might be a bad idea."

"Yeah, but it's what she knows," Exos reminded us. "She's going to feel safe there. And hopefully, she'll eat."

"We'll need to decorate." Claire was obsessed with her Christmas colors and seasonal items. "Can that be done before we go?"

"She might want to be involved," Cyrus pointed out. "Maybe we should wait and just have the items ready for her?"

Exos nodded. "Let's see what I can get done first, then we'll go from there. You focus on the Hell Fae. Titus, you keep monitoring Claire. Vox, see if River can't suggest a human remedy of some kind. And tell Sol to look into more fruit trees. And I'll organize our trip to occur during the solstice."

That would help us all out with missing work. As it was, I'd already delegated several of my courses to Lance because I had to make Claire a priority. But Vox didn't have anyone to share his course load with, and neither did Sol. Cyrus and Exos had the benefit of being their own bosses, so they could really do whatever the fuck they pleased.

"Right, I think we're set, then," Cyrus said. "I'm going to make arrangements for an underworld visit since that appears to be the only way to get through to Lucifer."

Exos gave him an uneasy glance. "You sure you want to do that?"

"I absolutely do not want to do it, but for Claire, I have to try," he replied. "Oh, were there any outstanding Shifter Fae we needed to track down?"

Exos shook his head. "The majority agreed, so it's a done deal. Kalt had the Winter Fae. Aflora already helped with the Midnight Fae. Same with Gina and the Fortune Fae. And most of the other breeds have also agreed, too. So it's really just the Hell Fae."

Cyrus grimaced. "Great. Well, wish me luck. I'm going to need it."

"Try not to get burned," I said, which was my version of *Good luck*.

The Water Fae snorted. "Thanks, Firefly."

I rolled my eyes. "I fucking hate that nickname."

"Which is why I will forever use it."

"And I'll forever call you a Royal Jackass," I drawled.

"One of these days, you'll scream that while I fuck you."

"In your dreams," I tossed back.

"Every fucking night," he agreed, smirking at me. Then he misted out of the room without another word. Typical Cyrus.

"Can you find River for me?" Vox asked.

I nodded. "Yeah, I'll go see if he's hanging around Water Quad." He was a professor now for human studies but spent most of his time with his kind. "Be back soon."

"Thanks, Titus," Vox said, his voice underlined in exhaustion. He'd been sleeping about as well as Claire.

"We'll figure this out," I told him.

"I hope so," he replied softly. "I really hope so."

CLAIRE

A WEEK LATER

EVERY DAY, I asked about the Hell Fae.

And every day, Cyrus assured me that I had nothing to worry about.

I didn't believe him, but I also didn't *want* to worry. As much as the vote mattered to me, the life growing inside of me took precedence. I couldn't shake the urgency that I needed to prepare and relax. Pretty soon, we'd all be busy with a little faeling in need of our love and attention.

"What are you all up to?" I asked. My mates had guided me away from the intended direction of my office and toward the neutral grounds at the center of the campus.

"You'll see," Cyrus answered cryptically.

I frowned. We usually only ventured over here to spar in the gym or take the portal to the Human Realm. My current physical state confirmed the former was out of the question, and the latter would only make sense if we were going into the Interrealm Fae Council area for the vote—which wasn't for a few more weeks.

An emissary waited for us as we arrived. Exos

greeted him by name, handing him payment in exchange for a beautiful coat with fur puffed around the lining. "You'll need this," he said to me, his smile wry as he handed me the present. "Let's try it on, shall we?"

"Won't I get warm?" I asked, narrowing my eyes at him.

His eyes sparkled. "Don't you trust us, princess?"

"Maybe I would if you told me where we're going," I said while I allowed him to wrap the impossibly soft coat around my shoulders.

It must have cost him a fortune. Because the emissary was from the Human Realm. It was the same one who brought Exos and Cyrus their tailored suits. However, when the coat wrapped me in suffocating warmth, I wondered if he was trying to sweat some sort of truth out of me.

"Patience," Exos murmured, using his favorite phrase.

"You're going to love it, Claire," Vox promised, sweeping my fingers up with his to press a kiss to my knuckles.

"Don't spoil it," Sol warned, then frowned at my languid pace. "Are you doing okay, Claire? Do you want me to carry you?"

I glanced down at my boots, aware that they hid my swelling feet.

It felt like my body had doubled in size over the last week. I wasn't exactly huge, just, well, a lot bigger than I used to be. And... "I'm tired," I admitted out loud. "And hungry. And now I'm warm." The last comment was for Exos.

I squeaked when Sol swooped me up into his arms without warning, making me giggle as I wrapped my arms around his neck. He smiled at me, his earthy eyes sparkling with mischief.

Really, what were my mates up to?

"You're *more* than tired," Exos said, opening the door to the realm travel chamber. "You're exhausted, which is why we're mandating you go on maternity leave—starting now."

Cyrus and Vox hid their pointed ears with their hair, while Sol, Titus, and Exos put on hats. Cyrus gave me a kiss as he tucked my hair around my ears as well.

Okay, call me intrigued.

My eyes lit up when Sol brought me into the room, and Vox turned on the portal, activating a sequence of buttons that brought festive Christmas music ringing through the air as it connected to its destination.

I recognized the melody instantly because I'd heard the same carols growing up.

Home. They remind me of home.

My eyebrows lifted. "Are we…?" I couldn't finish the hopeful statement, my heart beating a chaotic tune in my chest that reminded me of that famous song about bells.

"We think we know why you're not feeling well, little queen," Cyrus said, keeping his tone soft while the Christmas music lingered in the air. The atmosphere hummed as the world around us distorted, the smooth realm transition taking place in one of the more secure transit devices built by the Fortune Fae.

"What's your theory?" I asked, a smile hinting on my lips as I waited for the realm travel to complete so I could see exactly where we were going. I hadn't been back to my hometown in ages. I could almost taste the hot chocolate from my childhood. Although, my childhood had often been a lonely one.

Sol shifted me in his arms, keeping my belly resting

comfortably against his chest while Cyrus leaned in and pressed a kiss to my lips. His water magic tingled over me, reassuring me that I wouldn't be alone this year.

"You're half-fae"—Cyrus's blue eyes sparkled with magic—"but you're also half-human. And we think you might be in need of some human indulgences. So that's exactly what we're going to give you."

My lips curled. "I think you might be right. I've been craving my human food…"

"Why didn't you tell us?" Vox asked, his silver-rimmed irises flashing with a mixture of emotions. "I would have tried, Claire."

"I know. But you all have been doing so much… I didn't want to ask… It's… I've been okay."

Sol grunted at that. "*Okay* is not the word I'd use, Claire."

"You should have told us," Vox added.

"She's telling us now," Exos interjected. "That's what matters." He leaned in to brush a kiss against my forehead.

My heart fluttered in response. *Thank you,* I said to him.

He gave me a smile. *Anything for you, baby.*

This is exactly what I need, I promised. *Home.*

I loved my fae. I loved everything about their world, but with a child on the way, a sort of nostalgia gripped my heart and wouldn't let go.

I wanted my child to know everything there was to know about the world. Not just about the fae realm, but about where I came from, too. Humans had a good side to them, one I had enjoyed in my friends before my universe imploded. My child would be one-quarter human, and that was a part of our bond that I wanted to share.

The room shuddered as we arrived in the Human Realm, the doors opening onto a busy street just a few blocks from where I'd grown up. *Oh!* I smiled to myself. *Everything's just the way I remember it.*

I drew in a delighted gasp as Sol took me out into the open and a snowflake landed on my lips.

Winter.

Not just the fake kind with my attempts at springy cotton strewn about my office. *Real* snow landed in puffy balls all around me, making me feel like I'd stepped into the center of a snow globe.

This was what I'd been missing.

The cold drifted around me with its welcome embrace, and the coat Exos had given me did a good job of keeping me warm. I tucked my chin into the fur's edge and smiled.

Carolers strolled along the street, their songs highlighting the festive ambience. It made me want to dance and sing along with them. "Oh, Sol, put me down," I begged.

He appeased me, but not without a warning frown. "If you stumble, I'm picking you up again."

I promised him I'd be fine while I crunched my way through the snow, now grateful for the boots Cyrus had insisted I put on earlier. They weren't practical in the Elemental Fae realm, but now I understood why he'd wanted me to wear them.

"Your surprise is this way," Cyrus said with a smirk.

"This isn't the surprise?" I asked, my eyes wide. Just being here meant the world to me.

Titus rolled his eyes as if my question insulted him. "Please. Do you think just a realm jump is all we had in mind?" He took my hand and guided me down the street, ignoring the humans that stared at us. While my fae could technically blend in, they couldn't hide how otherworldly and freaking gorgeous they were.

"They're staring at you, not us," Cyrus corrected me, hearing the direction my thoughts had gone.

The side of my mouth lifted up in a wry grin. "Because I'm starting to look like a snowball with this growing stomach?" I guessed. "I'm painfully aware of how big I'm getting. You all have been kind not to comment on it."

Cyrus rested a hand on my belly, his love seeping through me along with his magic. "Everyone is watching you because you're radiant, Claire."

Agreement surged through my mate-bonds, reassuring me that I wasn't the walking marshmallow I envisioned myself to be. To my mates, I was the picture of beauty and fertility. That thought made me lift my chin with pride.

When we passed through the main streets from downtown into the more rural area, puddles formed where the city had oversalted—something about my hometown I'd forgotten.

Sol held out a hand, stopping me before I stepped into one of them by accident. Then he glanced at a car that blocked the higher ground and stormed up to it, gripped it from the bottom, and lifted it over his head.

"Sol!" I shrieked while Cyrus rubbed his temples.

My earth mate blinked at me. "What?"

Vox glanced around before sending a gust of wind magic to push the car off of Sol's shoulder. It looked as if it might crash to the ground, but Cyrus swept a layer of snow underneath it to cushion the blow.

Exos patted Sol on the shoulder, my Earth Fae mate still confused about what had just happened.

"There are rules in the Human Realm," Exos

explained, his words holding more patience to them than I had right now. The last thing I wanted was for interrealm laws to be broken when I was about to give birth.

The consequences were dire—a necessary measure to keep fae from revealing themselves to non-fae species.

The Human Realm was one of the last remaining neutral zones. Thus, fae valued humans in a variety of ways, and many of those benefits would be in jeopardy if the non-fae ever found out how they were being used.

It was a bit strange to think that way since I used to be human. Well, I wasn't truly human. But half-human and unaware of my heritage.

Anyway, the train of thought was so natural now, when it used to be quite foreign.

But maybe humans shouldn't be taken advantage of so—

Relax, Cyrus demanded in my thoughts, the word an order. *You're here to rest, not to devise more political schemes.*

I glowered at him. "I am relaxed," I said out loud and stormed through the puddle. I could rest and scheme at the same time.

Cyrus whispered the puddle away from my steps, casting it out like a mini tidal wave that froze in beautiful arcs.

I rolled my eyes. "Now who's risking breaking interrealm laws?"

"Nobody's around," he said, his voice cheery as he guided our little group around the corner. "That's why we picked it. We want you all to ourselves."

I gasped when I spotted what he meant. A darling cottage rested at the end of a long trail of snow, filled with a field of browned cornstalks in neat rows behind it.

"Do you like it?" Cyrus asked.

Tears filled my eyes and tumbled over my cheeks. I sniffled and wiped them away with the back of my hand, but they kept coming and soaked into the fur lining of my coat. "Oh, Cyrus—all of you. Yes! Yes, of course I love it."

"She's crying again," Sol said, sounding distressed. "I don't like it when you cry, little flower."

"I'm fine," I promised, slipping my hand into his and giving him a squeeze. "Really. These are happy tears."

My mates stood around me like a protective barrier, blocking off the harsh wind that slipped through the open area. Cyrus didn't look convinced that I was okay; he didn't like my tears, either, but he didn't chide me for it, and we all walked to the cottage.

This felt right.

A jump inside my stomach agreed, making fresh tears come as I realized that the first things my faeling would experience would be all the things I loved about home.

SOL

A FEW DAYS LATER

I HELD up the strange leafy cone Claire had given me. She claimed she was going to teach Vox how to cook it, but it didn't look all that edible. "What's this called again?" I asked, testing it with my teeth. It gave way with a hard *crunch*.

"Sol!" Claire cried out, grappling at my arm and snatching the leafy cone from my grip. She bounced back onto her stool we'd brought into the kitchen so she could stay off her feet while she showed us human food. "You have to peel the husk, first," she instructed as she ripped off one of the sides, revealing a strange, yellowish, pebbled texture underneath.

I lifted one lip. "It looked better with the leafy cone."

Claire giggled at me. "It's corn, silly," she said as she took a white, oily stick from the refrigerator and swiped it over the *corn*.

I raised an eyebrow and glanced at Vox, who just shrugged. "So, is this popper corn?" I asked, looking over her shoulder. "You'd mentioned something about that for snacking." I liked snacks.

She pointed at a canister on the counter. "No. That's

popcorn in the tin." She bit her lip. "I hope that one's fresh. I know you just picked it up from the store, but can you check the date on the bottom, Vox?"

He did as instructed, picking up the canister and peering underneath it. "I see some squiggly numbers."

Claire asked about the last two, which she said indicated the year, and determined it would be safe to eat.

Curious how this popper corn would taste, I left Claire lathering her yellow pebble cone with the white stick while I opened the canister and chomped on a handful of the stuff. This time the crunch was even louder, but the taste was satisfying.

"No, Sol." Claire choked on a laugh, nearly toppling over her stool as she tried to jump to her feet. She grabbed her stomach, her instincts seeming to kick in to protect the baby from the nearby counter. "You're supposed to pop it, first."

"I'll make sure he doesn't eat any more of your ingredients," Vox promised, guiding her back to her seat before giving me a glare.

"How was I supposed to know? I don't even understand how these things pop?" I complained.

"Stop stressing her out, you walking mountain," he muttered. "You're ruining it."

"Am not," I grumbled back, earning a curious glance from Claire.

"Of course you're not," she said, smiling cheerfully. "Can you fill up that pot, Vox? The cobs are ready to boil."

Vox gave me one more glare before he shoved a pot under the faucet and filled it. "This is for boiling the corn sticks? And then we'll have a separate pot for the ones we have to pop?"

She chuckled, although I wasn't sure what she found funny. "Yep."

I folded my hands in front of me and stood in the corner, resisting the urge to eat more of the raw popper corn. It had tasted just fine to me. Not sure why it needed popping.

I zoned out while Vox and Claire worked, and instead listened in on Cyrus and Exos arguing in the background about the Hell Fae, with Titus adding his loud opinions—ones I matched.

Even though they had enough fae to support the Interrealm Fae Academy vote, Cyrus was insistent on needing the Hell Fae support. I understood why—to make Claire happy. But she didn't get how horrible those fae could be. They kidnapped their potential mates and forced them into deadly competition with each other. How could Claire want to be involved with beings like that?

I might not understand all of the ins and outs of interrealm politics like Cyrus and Exos did, but even I knew they were bad news. I had no interest in working with creatures like the Hell Fae and would rather smash their faces in for making our mate cry.

But Claire had a heart of gold.

And this was what she wanted.

Hence, the debate in the other room.

My nostrils twitched when I smelled something burning. I turned to find that the peeled leafy husks had gotten too close to the hot coils and were now on fire. My mate was the clumsy sort, but powerful in her elements, so I didn't jump to her rescue.

Except she didn't use her fire magic at all, and instead she yelped in pain.

I stormed to her side, knocking over the dining room furniture in my way.

"Claire!" Vox yelled, sending his wind magic to push the flames down, working at them until they were sufficiently extinguished.

Claire hissed and stumbled into me, holding her arm as angry red splotches streaked across her skin.

I blinked. *It burned her?*

How was that even possible? She was one with the elements. Flames played over her skin all the time.

My chest began to burn, my lungs refusing to work. *Panic*, I recognized. *I'm… panicking.*

Shit!

The rest of our mate-circle practically ran into the kitchen, having overheard the commotion.

"What's wrong?" Cyrus demanded, his authoritative tone requiring answers. He rushed to Claire's side and saw the damage for himself. He glared up at me as if I were to blame. "How'd this happen?"

I opened my mouth to speak, but no words came out. I hadn't acted, leaving an opportunity for Claire to be injured. "It's… it's my fault," I finally managed to stammer out, my heart cracking in my chest. *I failed my mate.*

"It's nobody's fault," Claire interjected. "Well, nobody's fault but mine." She hissed when Cyrus sent tepid water over the burn, then relaxed as her skin began to magically heal through whatever royal voodoo he used to help her.

Titus frowned. "You need a Healer, Claire."

She shook her head as fresh tears came, causing my gut to twist in agony right along with her. "Claire—"

"I don't want to go back so soon," she said, cutting me off. "We've only been here a few days and—"

"Why didn't you use your magic?" Titus asked, his tone harsher than usual. He never interrupted Claire, but the anger in his gaze burned like hot embers. However, his rage didn't appear to be for her so much as for himself. It was his element that had caused her harm, and he hadn't been watching over her when it'd happened.

That was something I could relate to.

She bit her lip, then looked down.

"What is it, little flower?" I pressed, cupping her chin and lifting her gaze to look at me.

Her resignation stared back at me.

"My powers...," she began, then the tears came again. She sniffled and straightened, as if determined not to cry. "Nothing's wrong. I would know if something was wrong. I didn't want to worry you, I just..."

"You're rambling," Exos said, crossing his arms. "Start from the beginning, Claire. What's wrong with your powers? They're not working, right?"

"Not working?" I repeated.

"We talked about the possibility a few nights before leaving for the Human Realm," Titus explained. "But I think this is sufficient proof of our suspicions."

"You suspected her elements weren't working and didn't tell me?" My eyes widened. "What the fuck, Titus?"

"You were with Claire when we discussed it," Vox murmured. "And then I forgot to tell you about it. We were so consumed by the trip that..." He trailed off, his silver-rimmed black irises catching mine. "I'm sorry, Sol. I've been distracted."

"We've all been distracted," Exos murmured, his gaze on a trembling Claire. "When did you lose access to your elements?"

"I-I haven't been able to access the source since I became pregnant. And sometimes... I think... I think sometimes power is sort of coming out of me without my permission. Like the fire cupcake." Her hand fell to her stomach, running over it with a large, circular caress. The motion seemed natural, protective. "I think the faeling is blocking my powers somehow, but you said strange things could happen, right? I'm a Halfling, and nobody knows what to expect during a half-human, half-fae pregnancy."

Titus frowned. He liked this just about as much as I did. "You should have told us."

Her lower lip quivered, and I wrapped my arm around her, wanting to soothe her and throttle her at the same time.

It was just like our mate not to confide in us over something she would consider trivial. Or something she thought she was protecting us from.

"It's our job to protect you, little flower," I told her, squeezing a little. "We can't do that if you don't talk to us about *life-threatening* things." I glared at the others. "And you all are just as bad. If I'd known about your suspicions, I would have put out the damn fire."

"Vox already apologized," Exos said, ever the politician. "We should have told you. I'm sorry, too. But it's all out in the open now, right? Or is there more you need to tell us, Claire?"

"I just didn't want you all to worry," she mumbled, then looked up at me. "And I didn't want you to look at me like... like *that*. Like something's wrong with me."

I smiled and cupped her chin again. "We love you, Claire. We just want to make sure you and the faeling are okay. That's all."

She nodded, biting her lip. "Maybe… maybe I could visit a human doctor?"

Titus sighed. "I think a Healer would be better."

Cyrus considered Titus and then Claire. "Actually, I think a human doctor might not be a bad idea. It'll continue to soothe Claire's human side, which I think we all can agree is working. What can it hurt?"

He took Claire's hand, leading her into his embrace. I let her go, knowing that Cyrus would know exactly what to say to make her feel better.

He tugged her hair around her ears, hiding the pointy ends that gave away her fae lineage. "And if you want to use human technology to tell us the gender, I think that would be an amazing Christmas present." Cyrus must have picked that thought out of her head, because her eyes sparkled with excitement and understanding. He kissed her on the forehead, and I relaxed as her frown tilted upward into a smile.

"We can find out the gender?" Vox asked, a hopeful note in his voice.

"Yes," Claire whispered.

"Is that what you want, baby?" Exos cupped her cheek. "Do you want to know the gender?"

She bit her lip and nodded. "I do."

"Then so do we," Titus said, his gaze raking across the group to search for any disagreements. He sure as shit wasn't going to get one from me.

Excitement had replaced the discord in the mate-circle.

And that improved everything.

Is it a girl or a boy? I wondered, looking at her belly. I wanted it to be a girl. Preferably, a little fae sproutling who would one day blossom into a woman just as beautiful as her mother.

Or maybe that was what I wanted for us.

One day, I promised myself. *One day, we'll have a little girl.*

I felt certain of it, my lips curling into a grin.

Claire caught my look, her own mouth rivaling mine.

I would love that, she told me softly.

Me, too, little flower. Me, too.

CLAIRE

CYRUS HELPED me out of the rental car—one he'd picked up just yesterday on the off chance we'd need it—and escorted me into the hospital. He'd already said if the doctor found anything wrong, he'd immediately mist me back to the Elemental Fae realm—interrealm laws be damned.

I hoped it wouldn't come to that and instead filled myself with positivity and good thoughts as we walked through the massive hospital reception area.

Most people didn't like hospitals, but I found it amazing that there was a place I could go to and there'd instantly be people ready to help me. There was something to be said about human compassion.

Titus led the way while straightening the Santa hat I had gotten for him earlier at the store.

I tugged the white ball and grinned at him. "You sure do make a handsome fire elf."

He glowered. "Don't push it, Claire. The hat is humiliating enough with a ball dangling in front of my face." He blew the puff out of his way, glancing at a smirking Cyrus.

The guys had thought Titus should wear the hat to

keep the Christmas cheer going. My fire mate clearly didn't approve, which only seemed to amuse me, not upset me.

Yeah, pregnancy hormones were insane.

I sort of loved them.

A receptionist greeted us and helpfully pointed us down the hall.

Scheduling an appointment hadn't been easy, but there were benefits to having powerful mates. Exos had already established connections in Ohio prior to our arrival, knowing this visit might be needed. He'd also prepared for the potential birth—which I would want in a hospital, not at home. I loved that he thought ahead like that and that he'd do anything he could to make sure my wishes were granted.

We entered the office we were directed to, and another receptionist gave my group of mates a wary eye. "Uh, may I help you?"

"I'm here for my appointment," I said with a smile.

The woman blinked a few times at my mates, particularly settling her gaze on Sol, who had wandered to one of the seats and was trying to sit down —*unsuccessfully.*

"And, uh, who is the father?" she asked, keeping her head down as if this was a natural question to ask. "We prefer not to allow, um, visitors."

I frowned. Biologically, Cyrus was the father, but all my mates had a place in my heart, and in the life of my growing faeling. "They're all the father," I said without hesitation. "Is that a problem?"

A few women in the room coughed.

Exos leaned down, putting on the charming smile that he reserved for negotiation. He used it on me far too often—and far too often, he also got his way. "I've already spoken with Dr. Renalds. If you could please check with her, I believe she'll tell you everything is in order."

The receptionist twitched her nose and looked like she was going to argue, but Exos kept his perfectly constructed smile on his face, so she finally sighed and got out of her chair.

"Why is everyone staring at us?" Vox asked in a whisper as he rested a hand on the small of my back.

Yeah, there were a few details about human culture I hadn't missed.

"Polygamy is very uncommon here," Cyrus supplied. "In some countries, it's even illegal."

Vox frowned as if he didn't understand. "Why would a government control how many mates one can have? Do humans not sometimes have multiple soul mates like fae do?"

Exos cleared his throat as the side door opened and someone called my name. "Let's save the human lessons for later," he suggested under his breath before nodding to the nurse.

We all filtered through the hall, the staff giving my mates curious looks.

Titus lowered his hat around his eyes. "Now you like the hat," Cyrus mused, making my Fire Fae grin.

After a short wait in another room, and an awkward attempt at changing out of my outfit and into the pathetic sheet hospitals liked to call a gown, the doctor finally came in.

A tall woman with wild red hair caught up in a bun entered and gave me a bright smile. "Claire Summers, is it? And oh, you have so many fathers here to join us! I was intrigued when Exos told me about your situation.

You're from another country. He didn't mention which one, though."

Exos cleared his throat. "We're very grateful that you're able to see us on such short notice. I hope the hospital grant is still being put to good use?"

Her smile tightened, and I understood now why Exos had been able to get me an appointment on such short notice, as well as entry for all of my mates.

"Yes, absolutely. In fact, we were able to purchase two new sonogram machines, top of the line, one of which we'll be using today." She glanced at me. "Exos mentioned you might be interested in learning the gender of your baby?"

I beamed, glancing at all of my mates to confirm that they were dying to know just as much as I was. "Yes, we'd love to know," I said, sitting on the edge of the examination chair. "But first, I want to make sure he or she is healthy. That's all that really matters to me."

She nodded and wrote a note down on her chart. "Yes, of course. We'll do that right away."

She had me lie down, and my mates all found places to stand without being in the way. I knew none of this would hurt, but there was still a sense of anticipation anyway.

Vox and Sol looked at the machine that she rolled over, clearly fascinated with the technology. Cyrus and Exos had more experience with human machinery, whereas Titus was harder to impress.

The doctor swept a device over my stomach after slathering it with cold gel. We all jumped when a loud, rapid thumping sounded throughout the room. "Ah!" she exclaimed, zeroing in the device on the left side of my stomach. "There. Such a strong heartbeat."

My own heart seemed to speed up to match the rapid pace. "Is it supposed to be that fast?" I asked.

She smiled, her relaxed demeanor putting me at ease. "Yes. A fetus's heartbeat should be anywhere between one hundred and ten to one hundred and sixty beats per minute. Your baby is on the low end of the spectrum, but still in a healthy range."

My shoulders unhinged from my ears. "Okay, good."

"And the gender?" Cyrus asked, his tone hopeful. He likely already knew the heartbeat's pace and had evaluated the fetus through his spirit element, even if I hadn't been able to. But I suspected Cyrus had resisted from finding out the gender through his fae abilities. His gaze met mine, full of excitement, along with the rest of my mates. I knew this was a moment we'd remember for the rest of our lives.

She pulled out a different device this time, and a blotchy image appeared on the screen. She moved the scanner around on my stomach, making the baby inside squirm, but I couldn't sense distress, just a reaction to the pressure. The doctor smiled, and she clicked a button, outputting a still image that looked like an ink splotch to me.

She pointed at the screen. "See that? Looks like you're having a boy."

Titus jumped to his feet with a celebratory roar. "Yes! I knew it!"

My mates all likewise laughed, delighted in the news in their own way. As for myself, the awful tears came again, seeming to flood my vision no matter if I was happy or sad. I would have loved news of either gender, but a boy?

A boy.

A little fae king.

The thought made my heart swell three times over, and I thought I'd die right there on the spot.

I held Cyrus's hands in mine as the tears freely streamed over my cheeks. "A boy," I repeated the thought out loud.

Cyrus echoed my delight in my mind.

Our little holiday heir.

EXOS

December 23rd

THE MATE-CIRCLE practically hummed with excitement and the desire to celebrate.

Claire and the baby were fine—more than fine—and they would be even better after they were fed and sated.

Although, we planned to surprise our mate in more than one way in that regard. We all wanted to assure our Claire that carrying a child only made her more beautiful and more desirable, not less.

I glanced down at the list Claire had given me of human food items. When I told her I was going out to run some errands, she hadn't realized that included yet another detour to the Hell realm. Cyrus had ventured down there yesterday, and today had been my turn.

Those demon bastards were really giving us a hard time. And I was pretty sure it was purely for their sadistic enjoyment.

However, I felt pretty confident that we were making decent headway.

Rather than tell Claire about my little side trip—there was no benefit to worrying her—I'd just agreed to her errand, which was how I found myself strolling through a human market after spending a few hours in literal hell.

I roamed the aisles and grabbed every item on her list, plus anything else that looked interesting. I also grabbed some festive decorations for the cottage—I suspected Claire wouldn't mind adding to what we'd already put up.

Most of the food seemed unhealthy to me, but she could indulge. No, she *needed* to indulge. Growing a faeling required ample energy, so Claire needed as many calories as she could physically ingest.

After food, she needed to relax and rest, and I knew just the thing to distract her from thinking about politics and our faeling's impending arrival.

Every birth was unique, as well as difficult—that, unfortunately, ran similar between fae and human pregnancies. I'd done my research before going into this venture with my mate-circle to be as prepared as we could be for the unknown.

However, none of my planning could have prepared me for the protectiveness radiating through me, in addition to the new layer of love that threaded through my bond with Claire and our entire mate-circle. It brought us all closer together, knitted our love tighter, and gave it a sense of permanence that I hadn't realized had been lacking.

If one child did this, then I looked forward to many more.

After we survived this one.

And after Claire decided she was ready, of course.

For now, I would make sure she was as comfortable as possible and that she wouldn't have to worry about anything.

I finished my purchases and piled all of the bags into

the car, then headed back to the cottage. When I arrived, it was to find Claire laughing, the sound music to my ears and making my lips curve up on the sides.

Vox and Sol had positioned her onto a plush sofa with her feet resting on an ottoman. She looked like the picture of a fertility goddess mixed with North Pole magic, one of the only fae realms that humans had somewhat worked out, even if they considered Santa a myth.

I couldn't help but feel festive myself as I smirked at the snowflakes Cyrus had lured in from outside. He'd permanently frozen them, and Vox used his air magic to swirl them around on a loop, providing a festive flair for us all to enjoy. Titus also had several candles flickering in the windows, all using real flames —which would be a hazard for most humans, but not a Fire Fae.

In addition to our own decorative magic, we'd found human tinsel, holly, and red ribbons to place all throughout the interior. A single massive Christmas tree glowed near the window, adding its final touch to the ambience.

Claire grinned as I entered, then Cyrus joined me in bringing in all the groceries. Meanwhile, Vox and Sol argued over who got to massage Claire's elegant feet, which were poking out from the blanket she'd snuggled into.

"I'm much better at massages," Vox insisted, demonstrating on Claire's left foot. She groaned as he expertly swiped his thumb and worked at the swelling of her ankle.

Sol frowned. "We'll see about that. Is this the start of another challenge for faeling number two? Because I'm up for practicing."

"Don't count your fae before they hatch," Claire chided, making Sol's frown deepen.

"You're not going to lay an egg, Claire." His eyes grew big. "Right? I mean, do humans normally lay eggs?"

She chuckled as she eased further into the sofa. "No eggs," she promised. "It's just a phrase."

"Humans have strange phrases," Sol complained. After all these years, some things that our mate said still confused him, but he enjoyed learning.

"A massage trial would be just for practice," Vox coaxed, swiping his fingers again, working at a spot near her heel that had her biting her lip.

Oh, she knew where this was going. I could see it written into her flushed cheeks and the way she subtly arched her chest. *Beautiful*, I thought, momentarily distracted from putting away the groceries. Then Cyrus nudged me with his foot, and I took two bags from him while he ran out to grab more from the car.

"As long as we're not practicing the orgasm trial again," Claire said, her hands sweeping over her rounded stomach. "I think I'm still recovering from the last session." Even though she protested, her eyes sparkled with the memory, and a whisper of need swept through the mate-bond.

Yes, my Claire was ready for what we had in mind for tonight. I wasn't the only one reacting to Claire's growing desire to be physically sated on every level.

I'd been ready for this. Heightened libido was a trait both humans and fae experienced during pregnancies. Although, fae definitely experienced it at a whole different level—something Claire would be finding out very soon.

She was a fae with an already accelerated sexual

state, which suggested phase three could drive her mad once unleashed. I just hoped she didn't try to suppress it.

Fae were sexual creatures, filled with passion. We possessed the strength and stamina required to link the elemental sources together to produce new life. It wasn't a simple physical act like it might be for humans. For the fae, children were just as much a spiritual creation as a physical one.

Sol smirked, catching on to Vox's antics. "We'll practice the massage trial, then," he decided out loud. "I'll start with this foot, then we'll massage more of you after you eat." He glanced at me, and I gave him a low nod of approval.

Titus swept past me and started helping me put the food away as Cyrus carried in the last of the bags. He grinned, sensing the building tension. We all knew what was going to happen tonight.

Well, all of us except Claire.

"I'm going to win this one," Titus vowed, referring to tonight's pending events. Phase three was all about elemental sharing... through sex.

"I'm confident," he added, placing a precooked ham on the counter beside some of the items I'd already set aside for our meal.

I smirked but didn't reply.

Because there was no way in hell he would last the longest out of all of us tonight. My money was on me or Cyrus. We'd both danced with the source of power before. We knew how to keep it balanced.

Of course, the third phase would throw everything we knew out the damn window. So it really was anyone's game at this point. And frankly, we would all win in the end because it meant coming inside Claire.

Vox glanced between our mate and the kitchen.

"Does anything need to be cooked?" he asked, clearly not wanting to give up his competition with Sol's foot-massaging efforts.

I chuckled. "Most of it is precooked or packaged. We can handle the preparations, Vox. You don't have to always prepare our food."

Claire hummed in agreement. "Yes, you'd better not stop what you're doing. I command you to be the official foot-massaging mate."

Sol took that as a challenge. He'd learned how to control his strength over the years and demonstrated his skill by carefully kneading Claire's other arch with just the right amount of pressure, based on the way her eyes rolled back in her head.

"Correction," she said. "Both of you can be my foot-massaging mates."

My lips curled. "We'll let you know when the food is ready."

EXOS

CLAIRE'S EYES widened as we brought the trays of food to her, placing them all around her so that she wouldn't have to move from her chair. I'd found a breakfast tray that worked perfectly to perch food at eye level without disturbing her growing stomach.

She scanned the offerings as she licked her lips, the motion going straight to my dick.

Yes. Sex was absolutely what she needed tonight.

As well as the human food.

Already, she appeared healthier and happier, and well on her way to phase three.

We all sensed it coming.

Tonight.

She plucked at a miniature cake with white cream in the middle and moaned as she took a bite, making my pants suddenly tight.

"Claire," Cyrus warned, his lips lifting in a sly smirk. "If you keep making sounds like that, you're going to make us want to eat something, too. And it won't be food."

An adorable blush flushed over her cheeks as she chewed. "I can't help it," she said around a mouthful as she grabbed another item. "I'm just starving, and this is fucking delicious."

Mmm, I like that word from your mouth, I told her. *Say "fuck" again.*

Her gaze sparkled at me. *Fuck.*

I smiled. *Good girl, Claire. I'll reward you later for that.*

Don't make promises you don't intend to keep.

When have I ever not followed through on a sexual promise? I asked, arching a brow.

That had her flush creeping down her neck to disappear beneath the mountain of blankets.

I allowed her lack of a response, mostly because she made another moan as she bit into her cupcake again, and I couldn't think of anything else other than that sexy little sound.

All of us watched her eat, our own appetites growing with each passing minute. She seemed completely oblivious to the intensity, too lost to her meal. Which was good. She needed the energy for phase three.

But the new thread pulsed among us all, the life inside her tugging on our sources with such urgency that it couldn't be ignored any longer. The elemental source called to my affinity for spirit, urging me to bring the life in her womb to fruition by sharing my magic through our bonds on an intimate level.

I usually watched.

I usually waited.

This time… I wasn't sure I could.

When Claire had sufficiently sated her appetite for food, she leaned back with a contented sigh. "I feel much better," she admitted. Her eyelids drifted closed as her hands roamed over her stomach, smiling when her fingers twitched. "The faeling is kicking. He's happy, too."

And probably growing, I thought.

She'd slip into a preparatory sleep, soon. I sensed her closing in on the end of the final stage, the one where another mating would be required. It was an indescribable sensation of anticipation in the mate-bond, one that drove me to resolve that lingering requirement that plagued my mate.

While her appetite for food had been sated, I spotted the fleeting frown that crossed her face as her eyelids fluttered open to glance at us. She still had one need left to be met.

Or rather, five needs, judging by how her gaze scanned the mate-circle.

I removed the breakfast tray and Claire's blanket, then took her hand. "I believe we have a massage trial to practice," I said, my lips lifting with a mischievous smirk.

Her eyes sparked, but then she frowned as she grabbed the edge of my suit collar and sniffed. "Have you been smoking?"

Oops. Underworld problems.

"No, but I walked by some people who were smoking when I was picking up all the human food you asked me for," I said, casually reminding her that I'd gotten everything she'd requested on her list. And it wasn't a lie. I had walked past humans who were smoking, although they'd been on the other side of the parking lot. I kissed her cheek. "Are you ready for a massage, Claire?"

Her fingers closed into fists as she looked down at her stomach. "I don't think I can…" She knew what I meant, and it terrified her. I felt her fear surge through the mate-bond, and it twisted my heart until I could choke on it.

Cyrus joined me, taking her other hand to lift her to her feet. "You don't have to do anything, little queen."

His confidence seeped into my spirit, reassuring me that Claire could be convinced. We'd never failed before. "Let us adore you," he said, his tone sweet and regal. "That's all we ask."

She bit her lip before giving us a nod, which was all the permission I needed. Her spirit called to mine with such clarity that a melody unfurled in my mind, one where our souls danced together and began a new courtship.

Beautiful.

Cyrus and I escorted her to the massive bed, then I stopped her beside it. "Can I strip you, Claire?" I asked. "Massages are best when naked."

She licked her lips, then slowly nodded her head.

"Words, baby," I murmured. "Give me words."

"Yes," she whispered. "You can strip me."

I smiled and rewarded her with a gentle kiss, my fingers teasing the edge of her nightgown. "Thank you, Claire," I said, loving the act of removing her clothes. So did all the others, but I wanted to remind her with my words and touch, to ensure she felt just as beautiful now as she ever did before. Because to us, she was perfect. Gorgeous. A goddess of the elements, even if they were blocked right now.

Goose bumps pebbled her arms as I slowly pulled the strap of her gown downward. Then she froze as the material revealed her breasts.

Mmm, no, that wouldn't do.

I wanted her fluid. Warm. Aching for our touch. Not chilled and afraid of what we might think of her beautiful form. I could sense that uncertainty in our bond, had heard it in her voice when she claimed that she might not be able to accept a massage.

Our mate needed to go into phase three feeling cherished and loved.

Not unconfident and alone.

Could she not feel the pull from the source? The very real melody humming in my ears and in my heart and through my soul, begging me to take her? To fulfill the next stage? To give her what her body craved and desired most?

Oh, Claire.

I trailed my lips along her shoulder, urging her to relax, and brushed her spirit with mine, coaxing her closer to the blinding source of our power. A new life had been created here, one that we would cherish together as a family.

But first, she had to know how much she was loved by us all, how much we would always desire her. A child didn't change this facet of our lives. If anything, it only brought us all closer together.

"Lie down," I commanded, earning a feisty spark of rebellion in her eyes. She didn't like to be ordered around, but in this case, she needed to listen to me. She was far too wrapped up in her own self-doubts and fears. I needed her to let go and to give me control right now.

She righted her nightgown, hiding all the luminous skin from us, but lay down on the bed like I'd demanded. I knelt beside her and ran my fingers down her cheek. "I need to love you, Claire."

I rarely begged, and that was as close as I was going to get to it. She bit her lip before replying. "Well, lying on my back is actually a bit uncomfortable," she admitted.

I smirked. Oh, well then, I had another position that would suit even better for my mood. "Can you rest on your knees?" I suggested, one eyebrow lifting as the plan unfurled in my mind. "I was going to massage your breasts, but I can work with another area."

She swallowed and glanced at the rest of the mate-circle, taking note of how Sol and Vox rested near the wall, eager to have a good view of what was to come. Cyrus and Titus had eased around on either side of us, slipping onto the bed with sensual intention that dripped through the mate-bond.

I snapped my spirit magic through her, making her gaze jolt back to me. "But I'm so... *pregnant*," she protested, still doubting her beauty. As if the sight of her would dampen our love or deter our desire.

This was precisely why this needed to happen right here, right now.

"On your knees, Claire," I told her, allowing her to hear the demand in my voice.

She swallowed, but complied, her pulse thrumming so hard I could see it against her neck.

Words weren't going to solve this.

So we would lead with actions instead.

I eased into my secondary affinity for fire and smoldered a careful layer over her gown, disintegrating it and leaving her bare. The heat glowed pleasantly against her skin as she fisted her hands against her sides, still nervous and uncertain.

Determined to assure her, I followed my magic with my hands and then my lips, kissing her swollen breasts down to her enlarged stomach. Then I slowly pushed her forward to balance on her hands and her knees.

Cyrus and Titus waited patiently, their arousal evident. I had no doubt they could hear the same melody I did, the call of our elements too strong to ignore.

Our mate shivered as I swept my touch down her weeping sex. "Exos," she said, my name more of a plea now. I smiled. That was the right direction, but I needed more from her.

"What kind of massage would you like?" I asked, grabbing her ass with both hands as I spread her open for me.

Fae, she was beautiful. My cock lurched at the sight of her so wet for me, eager for my tongue to taste her sweetness.

Vox and Sol both made strangled sounds from behind me, likewise affected by the gorgeous sight, but not just that. Claire sent a wave of desire through us all that hit like a bolt of lightning.

There it is, I mused. *The third phase is coming.*

Exos...

Don't fight it, baby. Revel in it. Erase your fears and just feel.

I kissed the base of her spine, my palms branding her hips as I stroked her through her insecurities, encouraging her to come out and play.

You're our goddess, Claire. Our queen. Let us worship you. I nibbled her hip bone, then drew my tongue upward to her spine once more. *Please, baby. All we want is to make you feel good.*

She groaned, her worries slipping from her mind as she shifted her focus to the very real throbbing between her legs. I could feel it riding her spirit and pulsating into mine. She needed this. Just as much as we needed this.

Can you feel our need? I asked her. *Is it burning you the way your desire is burning me?*

Another groan, this one followed by her fisting the sheets.

Cyrus increased the intensity by unzipping his pants

and freeing his erection, his palm stroking the shaft in a leisurely pace as he watched her beneath hooded eyes.

Titus copied the motion, allowing our Claire to see what she did to him. To *us*.

"Do you see how hard they are, baby?" I asked against her ear, my hands still roaming her body, light and petting rather than thorough and knowing. I wanted her to cave first. Then I'd give her what she needed, what we *all* needed. "Is that precum, Titus? I think you should give our Claire a taste. Remind her how much we want her."

Titus swiped his thumb over the tip and brought the moisture to her lips. She moaned loudly in response, her body convulsing beneath my palm.

"Mmm, that makes me want to taste you, baby," I said, widening her knees to accommodate my shoulders as I lay down on the bed beneath her, my lower body still supported by my feet on the ground. "Sit on my face," I told her. "Let me taste you."

She shuddered, her legs wobbling beneath the intensity of my command and her overwhelming yearning to comply. Cyrus shifted closer, his fingers finding her nipple and giving it a little tweak. "My brother gave you a command, little queen. Are you going to disobey him?"

"I…" She trembled, her pussy lowering to my mouth, where I gave her a firm, long stroke with my tongue. "Oh, *Fae,*" she breathed, nearly falling forward. But Cyrus caught her with his palm against her breastbone.

I suckled her clit, making her cry out my name in that tone I fucking loved. I did it again, and she rewarded me with a full-body spasm.

"Oh," she repeated, her legs convulsing. "I need... I *need...*"

"Tell us what you need, little queen," Cyrus murmured.

"Yeah, sweetheart. Tell us what you want," Titus agreed, his tone low and warm as he fed her another swipe from his thumb.

I didn't see it so much as feel it through the bond, her pleasure mounting to a cataclysmic frenzy.

"Cock," she said. "Oh, now. I need it *now.*"

I nipped her clit, then slid out from beneath her as the others began to disrobe.

Cyrus and Titus took her first, their cocks already free and very willing to satisfy. She took Titus into her mouth, taking him down her throat before she grabbed for Cyrus and did the same to him.

And fuck if that wasn't the most beautiful sight I'd ever seen.

As much as I liked to watch, I wanted to take my mate first this time. "My massage wasn't over," I warned her. "I was only just getting started."

She glanced back at me as I unzipped my pants. Then she licked her lips as she angled her ass to give me a better view.

Yes, this was how I preferred my mate. Willing. Needy. Demanding. And *wanton.*

When I slid forward and coated my dick with her wetness but refused to stretch her open, she groaned with frustration and took Titus into her mouth again, this time so forcefully that he jolted.

He released a growl. "Careful, beautiful, or I'm going to unleash this load I've been saving right down your pretty little throat."

That only encouraged her to work him that much harder, likely taking his statement as a challenge.

I slipped my dick over her clit, making her hips gyrate over my sensitive skin. I'd make her come like this first, then I'd properly fuck her.

She popped off of Titus's dick when I thrust through her folds, her back arching beautifully. "I want to see Vox and Sol," she moaned.

The two fae had begun fisting each other, something they knew Claire would like, and would only prime themselves for her when it was their turn. I angled her so she could see them, and her eyelids grew heavy with desire. She liked to watch her mates play, something I'd never indulged in, but I understood the voyeuristic tendency because I enjoyed observing, too.

Sol put one fist against the wall as he faced Vox, their naked bodies giving us a profile view as Vox fisted his own dick, then slipped the same hand over Sol's. The throbbing between Claire's legs intensified at the erotic display, encouraging me to run my head over her clit again.

She screamed as she fell headfirst into an orgasm she'd clearly been holding on to for some time.

Naughty, Claire, I thought at her. *We're going to have to make you come all night now, just to make sure all those climaxes you've denied are rectified.*

Her body spasmed in response, causing a sensual wave to crash through the bonds.

The melody intensified, roaring through our connections with a vengeance, demanding that we release control of our elements—something we'd all learned *not* to do.

The third phase had officially begun, and it required all five elements, not just one or two.

There's a very powerful fae growing inside you, baby, I murmured. *He wants all our elements.*

All of them? she replied, sounding exhausted already. Then she flared with sudden power, her spirit humming through our bond as the final stage ignited.

"Oh, *fuck*," Claire breathed, that word so beautiful from her very sexy mouth.

"Yes, Claire. That's exactly what we're going to do," I confirmed.

She didn't seem to hear me, her instincts taking over as she scourged the demand through us, ripping us open until there was nothing left.

We had no choice but to comply, to break the very rule that had grounded us all since we were young faelings ourselves.

Unleash the elements.

Open the source.

Drown in ecstasy.

Claire took Titus deep into her mouth, destroying his chance to fight his elemental release. Then she wiggled her hips against me, coaxing my cock to come out and play.

I was a strong male fae.

But not strong enough to deny my mate.

I thrust into her quivering body, giving her what she needed and cursing as she squeezed the life out of my fucking shaft. Each punch of her hips tested my resolve not to unravel before we'd even begun.

Titus gave in to her, failing to restrain himself and his power, and groaned as he came. Cyrus grinned against the other fae's exposed throat, then pressed a gentle kiss to his pulse. It wasn't meant as a taunt so much as a tender gesture of understanding, one Titus seemed to appreciate as his head fell against Cyrus's.

I slowed my thrusts, drawing out my pleasure as Claire came down from her high, and the harsh demand of her melody eased off, sated by Titus's offering. The Fire Fae slumped onto the bed as he threw his head back on a curse.

Oh, he'd lost this game—to see who could hold out the longest—but I wasn't far behind him.

Cyrus took his turn next. Claire grabbed onto him like her life depended on it, suckling at his dick with renewed need as the melody kicked up again, eager to devour us all.

I followed her movements with my hips, rewarding her when she took my brother deeper. I didn't care if this mating destroyed me. It was the most fucking beautiful thing I'd ever experienced.

Sol and Vox continued to stroke each other as they watched us, their eyes on Claire as she threatened to achieve an orgasm that would take us all under with her.

This was new, *raw*, something different that I hadn't expected when I'd read about pregnant fae sexual side effects.

But I sensed the reason now, the link of our magic that drew in our power and fed her just as much as any physical nourishment would. Instead of fueling her body, we fueled the threads of her elemental power that would bring the life inside her to full term.

I would strip myself of all of my magic if need be to give Claire and the child what they needed, and so I fucked her with abandon, letting go of my control as I poured my power into her.

She gasped at the hit of unreserved magic, and all of the elements burst around the room as all the fae in our mate-circle followed suit.

Embers glittered in her hair.

Dusty motes of earth drifted around us.

And a warm breeze swept across my chest.

Then mist steamed in the air, and we breathed it in, sending our very life force into our mate as we slipped over the edge and didn't look down.

Take all of me, Claire, I told her. *Take every last drop.*

CYRUS

Fuck.

I could barely breathe, my heart hammering so hard against my damn chest I thought it might explode.

I was pretty sure Claire just tried to kill us through fucking. And honestly, I wasn't even a little bit upset about it. Because wow.

That had been some of the most intense sex of my existence. As soon as I rediscovered my ability to move, I wanted to do it all over again. But she'd pretty much just sucked the water element out of me, leaving me dry and weak in her wake.

Thank fuck we'd done this in the Human Realm. I couldn't even imagine the repercussions of doing that at home, where we were all that much more connected to our sources.

Perhaps that was why she'd reacted so negatively to fae food. On some subconscious level, she knew where she needed to be for phase three.

Or it was all a twist of fate.

Regardless, it was right. And we'd survived. *Barely.*

Happy Christmas Eve, little queen, I murmured to her. Technically, it was Christmas Eve morning now. But as she couldn't hear me, it didn't really matter.

I took a calming breath.

Then joined her in the land of sleep.

"THANK. FUCK."

Exos took the words right out of my mouth.

Our third visit to the damn underworld had finally paid off, and I had the proof of it in my hand. Lucifer might not attend the vote, but I had his proxy letter, and that was all that mattered.

It had taken a little bit of negotiation, mostly because he'd demanded Elemental Fae females in exchange for his cooperation. When I told him that was never going to happen, he started asking for more practical things. Like help growing certain edible plants. And a few meant for getting high.

"I'm just glad it's done," I said, folding the letter into my suit jacket pocket. "I'm eager to return to Claire and repeat last night."

"Sounds like a good Christmas Eve to me," Exos agreed, punching the buttons into the portal board. Then he faced me with a grin as the system engaged to work its magic. "Titus wants a rematch."

"He'll still lose," I drawled.

"I know," Exos agreed. "But I won't."

I arched a brow. "You sure as fuck did last night."

"I wasn't prepared."

I grunted. "Fuck that. You're always prepared."

His lips curled. "True. I may have given in last night, but so did you."

"We all did," I replied. "She was fucking magnificent."

"She was," he murmured. "Which is why we need to do it again."

"Is it my turn to seduce her into it? Because I could probably complete that task faster."

"Only because of my help last night," Exos retorted.

I lifted a shoulder. "Not my fault you volunteered to go first."

"Yeah, yeah." He waved me off as we arrived in the Human Realm. "We need to think of more…" He trailed off, frowning.

I felt exactly what caused that expression to appear. *Something's wrong.*

I didn't ask permission, and Exos didn't hesitate. He knew what I had to do. I grabbed onto his wrist and accessed the reserves of my magic to mist us directly to the cottage.

While it was a short jump, misting outside of the Elemental Fae realm drained me considerably, and my vision darkened with black stars as I searched for our mate.

"Is she okay?" I demanded, unable to see.

If I fucking passed out when she needed me, I—

"*Cyrus!*" Claire cried out as she grabbed onto me, her tone panicked but her grip strong.

My vision cleared enough for me to see the source of her distress. She held on to her stomach, grinding her teeth as a wave of pain swept through the mate-bonds. *Labor,* I realized. *She's in labor.*

Claire immediately tried to shut us out in an attempt to save us from the agony, but I pulled her into my arms.

"Don't do that," I said, brushing away her hair. "Give us your pain, little queen. We can handle it."

We're here, I added into her mind. *You're not alone. We're all right here.*

CLAIRE

"I CAN'T DO THIS," I bit out as my mates hurried me into the hospital.

My water hadn't broken at all like they showed in the movies. It'd been more of a trickle. I'd honestly thought I'd lost control of my bladder, which had been embarrassing. But nope. It turned out that was the start of labor.

"You can," Cyrus assured me with a kiss as he guided me into a wheelchair. My mate still looked pale from misting in from wherever he'd been. I wanted to smack him and Exos for leaving, even if it was unexpected that I would go into labor early. What could have been so important to take that chance?

And on Christmas Eve?

The latest contraction eased off, and I released the breath I hadn't realized I'd been holding. Without the wave of pain overtaking my brain, I was able to think clearly.

Oh, right.

"Was today the vote?" I asked, my voice hoarse.

Cyrus and Exos shared a grin. "Not quite, little queen. But close."

"Well, tell me," I said, eager to know what had happened. They'd been out of the realm for a reason.

"Shouldn't we concentrate on the faeling?" Vox asked.

I narrowed my gaze at him. "I'm having a difficult time concentrating on anything else."

He flinched. "Sorry."

Titus pushed me into the elevator and stared at the buttons. "Which fucking floor was it again?"

"Third," Vox said, always efficient, as he shoved an arm through and stabbed the number. "That's triage, where they'll evaluate her."

"She's clearly in labor," Exos said, irritated. "What kind of evaluation do they need to do?"

"*Exos*," I said. "Tell me what happened."

"Pregnant and giving demands," Cyrus mused, leaning down to brush his lips over mine. "We were in the underworld, little queen. Lucifer has agreed to support your initiative, and I have his signed vote in my pocket."

My eyes widened. "You got the Hell Fae to—" I cut off on a gasp as pain crashed through me again, knocking the air from my lungs and causing all my muscles to tighten in agony.

I squeezed my eyes shut and tried to cut the pain off from seeping into my mate-bonds.

"I told you not to do that," Cyrus chastised as he took my hand. "If you can handle it, then we can, too."

When I opened my eyes again, all my mates had their hands on me, demanding that I share my burden.

This was something I knew no human birth could compare to. How many women could share their pain with those who genuinely wanted to help?

I hated to do it, but I knew none of them would

forgive me if I tried to shoulder the responsibility all by myself.

We were a mate-circle for a reason.

Forever and always.

And this was exactly why our links existed—*to help and support each other.*

I relaxed my constraints, allowing the mate-bond to flow through me as the pain dispersed through the circle.

All of my mates buckled, Sol in particular making the elevator jolt as he slammed into the side. "Holy fae," he bit out. "That's like getting hit by a mountain."

Vox groaned and rubbed his neck. "*Fuck*, Claire. You've been holding that in all by yourself? I'm with Cyrus. Don't take that on alone."

I grinned weakly, relieved as the pain lessened, much more manageable now that it was shared across the bonds.

The elevator dinged, and Titus pushed me out into the office. I pulled some of my discomfort back in to let my mates focus on signing me in. Then, the moment I passed triage and was cleared for the delivery room, I shared the aches and pains with my mates again.

Labor took much longer than I would have expected. I went through cycles of agony, in and out for hours. Every time the doctor came in, I wasn't dilated enough for delivery.

When we were left alone again for the umpteenth time, I turned to Cyrus. His silver-blue eyes watched me with concern. "Are fae supposed to dilate before giving birth?" I asked, wishing I'd spent more time talking with the Healers.

His lips curled on one side. "Yes. Be patient, Claire. Your body is still half-human. You've gone through an incredibly accelerated pregnancy for your genetic makeup. You can do this, but don't rush it."

"Patient?" I repeated. "You want me to be *patient?*" That was Exos's chosen phrase. Not Cyrus's. And I'd been pretty damn patient all night. "Why isn't my body cooperating?"

"Because you're not ready, Claire," Cyrus replied, his tone holding a touch of his trademark chastisement.

"But I was more than ready on Halloween when you *impregnated me,*" I snapped.

He sighed. "Claire. I know it hurts, but you're stronger than this."

My eyebrows winged upward. "Stronger? Are you…" I trailed off on a hiss as another contraction hit me. This one I blasted through the mate-bond, causing Cyrus to double over on an exhale. "Patient… enough… for you?" I asked through my teeth as another contraction hit me almost immediately.

Fuck! The shout came from all my mates. Or maybe one of them. I really couldn't tell because chaos had erupted around us as the doctors returned.

Sol and Vox were arguing about something.

Exos was speaking urgently to Cyrus.

And Titus was looking at me as though I were dying.

Am I dying? I asked him, panicking.

You're okay, sweetheart. I just hate seeing you like this.

"Claire," Cyrus was saying, pulling my attention back to him. "It's time to start pushing."

"What?"

"Push, little queen," he urged.

I'd completely missed where the doctors said it was time, but I read the urgency in their expressions.

"It's time?" I squeaked, then another pain slammed into my abdomen, and I about shot out of the bed.

"Cyrus!" He gave me his hand, and I clamped down, my insides rioting as my instincts took over.

Push.

Okay.

Push.

Yep.

I can do this.

But no matter how many times I pushed, it wasn't over, and all it did was radiate aches up through my hips and spine. It felt like I was being ripped in half, and not in a good way. "It's not working!" I cried out, anger and sadness and failure filling me as a hum sounded in my ears. "Why isn't it working?"

Cyrus and Exos sang into my thoughts.

Titus joined them.

Then Vox and Sol were there, too.

I barely heard the doctor talking over them, his voice so far away beneath the cloud of soothing evoked by my mates.

"I see the head," the doctor informed me. "One big push now on the next contraction. You can do it!"

I waited for the pressure to build, and then the pain hit again. That was my cue.

I screamed as a new burn ran through me, one of magic rather than physical torment. All of the elements that had been blocked unleashed at the same time, searing me with their raw power as if I'd touched the sources themselves.

Fire blazed across my skin.

Water crashed into the walls.

Air swirled in a violent spiral, kicking up the chairs and medical supplies.

The floor split, sprouting life all around us.

Pink butterflies burst into existence, glittering as they

fluttered through the writhing elements unleashed in the delivery room.

This wasn't me, but my *child*.

I didn't have time to process what this all meant. All I knew was that my son needed me right now to bring him into the world, and no matter if I died trying, I would succeed.

All of my mates placed their hands on me, calming the inferno of elements as one final push gave me the sweetest relief. I held my breath and stared up at the ceiling as the swirling of colors mixed together, releasing bursts of sparkles like stars.

Then a cry sounded.

My son…

He was finally here.

EXOS

"Congratulations," a dark voice whispered from the shadows of Claire's room. "The perceptions of the medical staff have all been altered."

I didn't know Shade well, but he came highly recommended by Aflora and Zeph. They told me if anyone could help us clean up this mess, it was the secretive Midnight Fae with a penchant for playing with time and memories. "Did Kyros help you?" I asked him, very aware of his close friendship with the Paradox Fae.

"If he did, I wouldn't tell you," he replied, his lips curling as he stepped out from the shadows. "But everything is as it should be."

I nodded. We'd already handled the elemental mess left behind from Claire's childbirth. Now she rested peacefully in the bed with her son cradled against her chest. Cyrus sat beside her, his fingers shifting through her hair as he closely watched Shade. Titus, Vox, and Sol all wore similarly guarded expressions.

Shade wasn't just a Midnight Fae. I could sense the otherworldly energy pouring off him like thick bands of wispy smoke, suffocating all those in his presence.

"Do you require anything else?" he asked, arching a dark brow, his icy gaze flashing.

"We just needed the memories altered," I replied.

He nodded and turned, as though to walk into the wall.

"Let us know what you want in return," I added, uncertain of what else to say to him. We barely knew each other, and he never attended the meetings with Aflora.

Shade glanced back over his shoulder. "I don't require anything," he said. "My mate requested a favor. And I never say no to my mate." His icy irises flashed again, an array of secrets brewing in their depths. "I have a feeling you understand."

"I do," I admitted.

"Good." He smiled. "Congratulations again."

With that, he vanished into the shadows. Literally.

I shivered, his inky magic leaving an imprint in the air that was severely at odds with my spirit essence. I had no idea how or why he'd mated Aflora, but it was clear that he worshipped the ground she walked on, which was good enough for me.

Sol, however, didn't seem to agree, his scowl firmly in place. "Willow stump," he muttered.

I arched a brow. "What?"

"Nothing," he grumbled.

"Mmm?" Claire mumbled, stirring from her rest and causing the baby to awaken against her chest. Rather than cry, he lifted big blue eyes up at his mother before staring straight at Cyrus.

My lips twitched. "Yeah, he's going to be bold."

"Of course he is," Cyrus cooed, smiling down at the little bundle. "He's a future king."

"King?" Claire repeated on a yawn, her long lashes fluttering open. "Oh. Yes. King. Hi there, little king. Oh, what a handsome little one you are." She positively beamed, her sole focus on the tiny faeling.

He blinked his eyes back to her, his love and adoration evident in the way he worshipped her with that intelligent gaze.

She cocked her head. "It's like he understands me."

"He does," Cyrus replied. "Faelings are a little different from human infants."

She slowly drew her gaze to Cyrus. "A little different, like 'nine-week pregnancies instead of nine months' different?"

I bit my lip to keep from smiling.

Cyrus, however, didn't bother to hide his grin. "Yeah, sort of like that."

Her eyes narrowed. "I want a better explanation than that."

"How about we name him first?" he offered. "Then we can talk about the differences."

I crept forward, very interested in this conversation now. Not that I wasn't amused before, but this took precedence.

"Name?" she repeated, swallowing. "Oh, I… In all our preparation… I…"

"Shh," he hushed. "I haven't thought of one yet either. I wanted to meet him first before I decided."

"Do you have one in mind now?" she asked.

"Sort of." He studied the faeling, his gaze intense. "He's our Christmas baby, born in the Human Realm beneath a wave of all five elements. So he needs a strong name, one that represents his birth and his elemental status. What do you think about Storm?"

"That's not very Christmassy," she said slowly. "But he did create quite the catastrophe on his way out."

"He came in like a rough storm, yes," my brother

agreed, his lips twitching. "I also thought of Frost because he created some ice on the ceiling that not even Titus could melt."

"He's going to be a handful," the Fire Fae said, his voice full of adoration. "I like Storm. It suits him."

"I like it, too," I admitted. "But I want Claire to love it."

She stared down at the baby. "What about Blizzard?" Her lips twisted. "No. That's too much. Hmm." Her expression turned pensive. "Jack is too plain. Winter isn't right, and Christmas doesn't fit."

"What about Ciro?" I suggested. "It's a variant of Cyrus, but it means 'of the sun.'"

Claire blinked at me, then down at the baby once more. "Ciro," she repeated, her expression brightening. "King Ciro."

"Prince Ciro," Cyrus corrected. "I'm still King Cyrus."

She beamed. "Yes, Prince Ciro. Oh, that's perfect. I love it." The baby seemed to agree, because he released a little giggle, which caused Claire's eyes to widen. "They can do that when they're this young?"

"Faeling," Cyrus reminded her.

But rather than demand he start listing all the differences for her, she just hummed in agreement and continued repeating, "Prince Ciro," to the little one in her arms.

Everyone smiled, pleased with the name.

And Cyrus turned his icy blue eyes up to me, a hint of emotion flashing in his depths.

He knew why I suggested that name.

It wasn't just because of the similarity to his name, but to Cira—our mother.

We rarely spoke about her, as she passed when we

were much younger, but she forever lived in our hearts. Just like our mate. And now, baby Ciro.

"Merry Christmas, Prince Ciro," our mate murmured, her gaze shining with tears as she looked up at all of us. "Merry Christmas, guys."

"Merry Christmas, Claire," we all echoed, dropping in to kiss her on the cheek and mouth.

"And happy birthday, Ciro," I added, giving the little one a nuzzle to his nose. "Now be a good boy and let your mom get some sleep. She's more than earned it."

CLAIRE

"I THINK we should go with the multicolor Christmas tree," Vox said, grinning at a sweaty Sol, who had just spent the last several minutes growing a selection of trees in our living room.

He'd mimicked the standard evergreen tree, then created one with pure white ferns similar to what was in our backyard, and finally a third one—his latest invention—a tree displaying multiple color pigments twisting along the branches. It really was impressive.

"The baby definitely likes multicolor best, right, Claire?" Vox glanced back at me, his silver-rimmed irises twinkling.

Of course, we didn't really need a Christmas tree for New Year's Eve, but Winter Solstice was in full swing back in the Elemental Fae realm, and I'd been rather occupied on our Christmas Day in the Human Realm.

Not that I was complaining.

Now that we'd returned to our Academy home, my son suckled at my breast, content as he made little sounds of enjoyment while I observed the tree-selection process.

"I'm afraid Vox is right," I told Sol, who still had a burp cloth on his shoulder—a permanent fixture he refused to remove. He loved holding the baby, and I wasn't one to deprive him of it. Whenever my arms grew tired, my rock was there to hold our son for me.

Sol gave me a soft smile. "You're lucky that you're pretty," he said as he leaned down and tapped the raw earth exposed through our ruined floor. He glanced at the babe at my breast. "And you're lucky that you're cute, Ciro." Then he sighed. "More trees coming up."

The ground trembled while Sol worked, and I chuckled, delighted by the display of reds, greens, yellows, and purples that shot out from the branches, a new trick I was intent on learning.

Cyrus and Exos entered the room, my water mate rubbing his temples. "Who let the Earth Fae loose again? I just had the floor repaired."

Titus walked in from the kitchen, shaking a bottle as he elbowed Cyrus on his way to me. "You act like you don't have the funds," he teased, then handed me the supplemental formula.

I pinched my breast to unlatch my son's mouth, then I readied the bottle sparking with embers in its milk. I smiled up at Titus, grateful that my mates continued to help me supplement magic for our son.

The baby complained until I offered the bottle's nipple, and then he latched on, making me chuckle. "Greedy one, aren't you?"

"Insatiable," Cyrus agreed as he came to me and kissed the crown of my head. "I can't imagine where he gets that from."

My lips curled, amused. "No idea."

His lips moved to my ear. "Aren't you going to ask where we've been?"

I blinked. "Why would I…?" My mouth dropped open. "Oh, Fae! Was the vote today?"

Cyrus grinned. "It was."

"Why didn't you remind me?" I demanded.

"You and Ciro were napping, and we didn't want to ruin it," Exos replied. "So we attended to oversee the vote."

I waited, but neither of them continued. "*And?*"

Ciro's nose scrunched at my tone, then he went back to sucking on the bottle a half second later. The little guy knew what his priorities were, just like my mates. Which was why I didn't get mad that they hadn't woken me. Because I probably wouldn't have wanted to leave Ciro anyway. It was too soon.

"The vote passed," Cyrus finally said, his lips curling. "No one voted against it. The Interrealm Fae Academy project can officially begin."

I jumped up in excitement, then immediately stopped as Ciro gurgled in response. It took me a second to realize he was giggling around his bottle.

Vox walked over, cooing at the little man, and took him from me so I could properly react, which included hugging Exos and Cyrus extra hard. Then kissing them within an inch of my life. And also promising a whole slew of dirty things in their minds.

"I'm holding you to that," Cyrus said.

"I would expect nothing less," I replied, grinning like a loon. "Oh, I can't believe it passed!" I knew they'd gotten the Hell Fae to somehow agree, but hadn't heard any of the details yet. Mostly because they'd delivered the news as I was going into labor. Still, I couldn't be more thrilled that they'd pulled this off for me. I really did have the best mates in the world.

"I told you to trust us," Cyrus murmured. "We're good at negotiating."

"I know," I deadpanned. "Very good."

"The best, actually," Exos said, his tone indicating he meant it.

Titus grunted, then took Ciro from Vox and started humming him a little fae ballad, his gaze filled with love and adoration for the now-grinning faeling in his arms.

I smiled, my heart bursting with warmth. All of my mates helped with every single task, even diaper changes. And I never even had to ask.

Seriously, I was probably the luckiest woman in the world. And it made me just so incredibly grateful for them and their support system and their love.

Just as I was grateful for my multiple Christmas celebrations as Sol finished his multicolored forest of trees. Cyrus took our son as Vox and Titus went to work adding magical ornaments, all of them glittering in the setting sun, something Ciro found just as mesmerizing as I did.

It really was a merry Christmas. My favorite one yet. "You guys are so screwed," I realized out loud, laughing. "There's no way another holiday will ever beat this one."

Titus's eyes gleamed with embers as Exos gave me a smoldering look of his own.

"Don't be so sure about that, little queen," Cyrus murmured. "This mate-circle is only just getting started."

EPILOGUE
CYRUS

TEN MONTHS LATER

"SO, WHEN ARE WE DOING THIS?" Titus asked, his eyes burning with intrigue. "Because we're definitely starting with the orgasm trial. I deserve a rematch."

I smirked, amused by Titus's confidence that he would win this time around. And maybe he would, but one glance at the rest of our mate-circle proved he was going to have his work cut out for him.

Sol sported his permanent burp cloth and a record for most bottle feedings. It seemed the fae's rumbling heartbeat put our son at ease.

Vox held the diaper-changing record, to which we were all immensely grateful.

Titus could always make the faeling laugh, even without trying. My son found his aggression amusing— just as I did.

Exos constantly knew what my son needed, regardless of what it was. His spirit had intertwined with the child, giving them a link through their mother that I adored.

And then there was me. I could always calm Ciro no matter his discord, able to lull him to sleep with a push of tranquility and peace—a gift that came to me whenever I thought of Claire.

If one fae child was like this, then I looked forward to more.

All of us were ready for round two. Except for maybe Claire. Which was why we'd devised a longer trial this time around.

"We tied on the orgasm trial, Firefly," I reminded him, enjoying his flare of aggression at the nickname.

Yes, I'd call him that until the end of time.

I loved fucking with him in every possible way.

"You're disqualified this time around," Titus informed me, his green eyes burning with challenge. He stabbed a finger at my chest, making me grin. "I don't think you should even get to participate."

Oh, I very much was going to participate, even if it wasn't for points. I didn't need an excuse to fuck Claire.

Igniting Titus was just a side bonus.

"I thought you wanted a rematch?" I taunted him.

His jaw ticked in response. "You're going down, Royal Jackass."

My lips twitched. "I only kneel for Claire."

"So you say," he replied. "But I'm going to change that. One day."

"In your dreams," I agreed. "Sure."

"Never—"

"We need different trials," Sol interjected, tapping his lip. "How about a gardening trial?"

"Like you wouldn't have an edge there," Vox said, rolling his eyes.

"An Elemental trial," Exos suggested. "One where each of us is tested based on our affinity." He crossed his arms and leaned against the wall of the empty nursery, sending a new flurry of purple butterflies to dance against Titus's drifting embers. "After the last phase three mating, I think a magical endurance trial would absolutely be in order."

We all shifted our feet as we recalled that experience. Yes, that was something I very much wanted to do again.

Claire cleared her throat, glowering at us as she dripped water onto the floor by the doorway. "I hope you guys aren't talking about what I think you're talking about. It's not fair to conspire when I drop our son off for a visit with his grandmother." She flicked her wrist, sending more droplets scattering. "He still has some serious separation anxiety. Fae help my mother, but that woman is a saint for watching him."

Titus slipped his arm around her waist, sending a lasso of flames to wrap around her chest. "Who can blame him? I don't like being separated from you either," he murmured. "Although, now that you're free, I suggest that I dry you off, starting by removing your clothes."

"Uh-huh," she said, lighting herself on fire to dry her own clothes. It served as a statement to remind us all that her elements were fully functional once more. "You can't distract me. I know what you're up to."

Well, that certainly sounded like a challenge to me.

Titus seemed to agree, because he nipped at her. "Our faeling needs a little brother or sister, maybe one who can keep his elemental affinity in check?" he suggested, referring to her previously drenched state. My son had learned how to splash his magic, and he particularly loved dousing us with the magical waves.

I loved it.

Claire, not so much.

"I'm not ready," she said, her words holding a flat tone to them as she accessed her fire magic to dry out her hair.

I scooped her into my arms, guessing that her reservations came from how many surprises she'd endured the last time. We certainly could have done a better job of preparing her for a fae birth, but I wouldn't make the same mistake twice. "We know what to expect this time around," I assured her, running my thumb along her lower lip. "I'm not saying it'll be easy, but we've proved that you don't have to do this alone, little queen."

She sighed. "Yes, you have. That's not the problem." She rested her cheek against my shoulder, her gaze growing distant. "I'm just afraid of neglecting him when a new faeling takes the spotlight, you know? I want my son to get all the love he needs."

Vox chuckled. "Claire. You have five mates who adore you, and you're worried about sharing your love?"

She pursed her lips. "I guess it does sound silly when you put it that way."

She held out her hand, taking Sol's extended fingers as she surveyed our mate-circle. She'd never left anyone out, and I knew she would be able to share her love with five faelings without any issue.

Maybe even more.

"Would you like to hear about the new trials?" I asked, trailing my fingers south. "I think you'll like them."

"Prolonged trials," she immediately said, spinning in my arms to face everyone else.

My eyebrow arched as I met Exos's gaze. His expression told me he had the exact same thought as I did.

She's already thought about this. Which meant she'd already accepted the inevitable, at least on some level.

Good.

That would make this much simpler.

"I'm still not ready for another faeling yet," she added. "Pregnancy and birth suck. You're going to have to convince me to do it again."

"You didn't enjoy phase three?" I asked against her ear as I settled my hands on her hips.

She shivered. "Okay, that… that doesn't count."

"Doesn't it?" Titus closed in on her front, running his finger down her chest, blazing a line that cut through her shirt. "Can we start working on the convincing now?"

"I…" Her lips parted when Vox and Sol came to her side, their hands roaming along her exposed flesh. "Maybe."

"Maybe?" Sol repeated, cupping her breast. "And how would you like us to convince you, little flower?"

"Orgasms," she breathed, arching into his touch as he pinched her nipple through the fabric. "Lots and lots of orgasms."

I pressed my arousal into her backside, fitting against her with the anticipation of meeting her every desire. "That can be arranged."

Titus growled, nipping at her throat. "And this time I plan on winning."

I grinned. "Then let the trials begin."

Claire released a sigh as I slid my touch south again to move her panties aside, allowing Titus the access he required. Perhaps I'd give him a head start.

Her legs quivered as she released a delicious whimper. "Well, happy holidays to me…," she said. "*Again.*"

～

The End

Curious about Kalt and his Winter Fae triad? Check out
Winter Fae Queen.

Want more Lance? You can read all about him in
Candela,
a Silver Springs why-choose story.

Other Fae World Series:
Elemental Fae Academy: The Complete Trilogy
Hell Fae: Dark Why-Choose Romance
Midnight Fae Academy: Vampire Why-Choose
Romance
Fortune Fae Academy: Omegaverse Why-Choose
Romance

A Note from J.R. Thorn

I want to thank you for reading Elemental Fae Queen and following Claire on her journey that has grown personal for me over the years.

After giving birth to my daughter the DAY that Lexi and I finished writing Elemental Fae Academy Book 3, this book was something that was on my mind all year and I couldn't wait to write it.

Birth is no picnic. Neither is the first year of your child's life. I wanted to write an escape where the difficulties of birth could be shared by five loving and attentive mates, who understood what Claire was going through and wanted to be there for her through thick and thin. I'm not saying my own husband wasn't there for me, but real life tends to pale in comparison to how you might imagine it.

So I hope you found an escape just as I did with Claire and her mates. May you have a Happy Fae Festivus Holiday, no matter the time of year you're reading this now. Until next time!

Love and Peaches,
Jen

Winter Fae Queen

The Royal Water Fae I'm in love with just hired me to be his intern.

Oh. My. Fae.

I only applied for the job because of a dare, and now I'm packing my bags for the North Pole.

No big deal. I can totally be professional. I haven't seen him since the Academy anyway. Maybe he's gotten fat from all the Winter Fae sweets?

Except, no. Kalt hasn't gotten fat at all. He's still perfectly chiseled and even more gorgeous than I remembered. And worse? He has two equally hot friends.

A royal elf named Lark.
And a sexy-as-sin selkie named Norden.

I am so screwed. And I mean that literally because the elf and the selkie seem to think I'm their mate. Only Kalt completely disagrees.

Oh, and not only am I dealing with these three hotties, but my water magic is also on the fritz. I accidentally stirred up a snowball fight in the middle of Santa's workshop, then ice tinsel started shooting from my fingertips like confetti.

It's a problem.
One I'm not sure how to solve.
So, yeah, wish me luck! And send warm vibes. I really need some help melting all this snow…

Winter Fae Holiday *is a quirky paranormal romance featuring a Water Fae from the Elemental Fae universe and her three potential mates.*

Candela

What does a firefighter, a Fire Fae, and a husky shifter have in common? They all want a bite of Candela's cupcake...

Hi! I'm Candela and I own the best cupcake shop in Silver Springs—before my reputation got ruined, anyway. Lately all of my cupcakes have been coming out burnt, my smoke detectors are on the fritz, and my husky companion named Jasper won't stop barking at customers. When I thought it couldn't get any worse, my favorite Christmas candle set my display stand on fire.

With no choice but to close up my shop for the day, I decide to release some stress at Silver Spring's skating rink. You'd think that would chill me out—wrong! Apparently I'm a magnet for trouble because I've been hit by a mate spell and now I'm trapped between three guys who all want a taste.

Shane—the firefighter who wants to start my fire instead of quench it.
Jasper—my husky who turns out to be a shifter… he took showers with me, the pervert!
Lance—a sexy-as-sin Fire Fae who said his brother Titus sent him to my world to recover fire magic that didn't belong to me and now its running rampant in Silver Springs. That sounds about right.

Send help, because these guys are going to burn me to a crisp!

Candela is a standalone paranormal comedy romance with a mystery to solve and a guest appearance of a delicious Fire Fae from the Elemental Fae universe—Titus's brother!

This story is part of the Silver Springs shared universe and can be read in any order.

Welcome to Elemental Fae Academy where fae are real, the mentors are hot, and a magical plague has wiped out entire kingdoms. Oh, and the fae think I'm to blame.

↳☆☆**Elemental Fae Academy: Book One**☆☆↰

I kiss one guy at a bar on a dare and suddenly I'm whisked away to the fae realm, thrown into an Academy to control my gifts, and dodging mean girls who want to pin me for crimes I didn't commit.

It's a lot to take in, but I have help and they're in the form of several sexy Elemental Fae mentors. They're supposed to help me control my powers, but who's going to keep the elements from controlling me?

↳☆☆**Elemental Fae Academy: Book Two**☆☆↰

Someone wants me dead and they're using my missing mate to get to me. I have to stop them before it's too late.

No big deal. Master the elements, find my lost Spirit, and identify the bad guy.

Yeah. Easy.

Except Titus is tired of playing by the rules of others. Vox just wants to be friends. Sol is pissing everyone off. And Cyrus, well, he's a force of nature and thinks he's in charge.

Whoever is out to hurt me and mine will pay.

↰☆☆Elemental Fae Academy: Book Three☆☆↲

Royal Coronations. Finals. A Solstice Ball. And a mother hellbent on ruining the fae world.

Just another ordinary day for me, Claire Summers, the halfling fae with access to all five elements.

I'm in for the fight of my life with five fae protectors and an ally I never saw coming. It's up to us to save the Elemental Fae Kingdom before it's too late. And it'll require giving my heart to all my mates, to guard and to hold, for eternity and beyond.

This is a Paranormal Romance Complete Trilogy where there are five hot fae mentors and no choosing required!

FIND OUT MORE ABOUT AFLORA, ZEPHYRUS, AND SHADE,
IN MIDNIGHT FAE ACADEMY...

Welcome to Midnight Fae Academy.
Home of the Dark Arts.
Vampires.
And cruelly handsome fae.

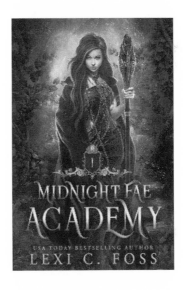

**A forbidden bite led to my capture and
recruitment.**

There are no flowers here.
No life.
Only death.

I'm an Earth Fae who doesn't belong here.
They can play their little mind games all they want, but

I'm going to find a way back to my elemental world.
Even if it kills me.

Except Headmaster Zephyrus is one step ahead of my
every move.
Prince Kolstov won't stop cornering me.
And Shadow—the reason I'm in this damn mess to
begin with—haunts my dreams.

My affinity for the earth is dying and being replaced by
something more sinister. Something powerful. Something
deadly.

The Midnight Fae believe this is my fate.
They claim that I was "recruited" for a purpose.
To battle a rising presence.
Or to die trying.

I don't owe them a damn thing. But if I have to pass
their trials to find my way home, then so be it. I survived
a plague and far worse in the Elemental Fae realm. An
ominous energy? Please. What a joke.

Give it your best shot.
I'm waiting.
And don't you dare bite me.
Or I'll make you regret it.

Author Note: This is a dark paranormal reverse harem
series with bully romance (enemies-to-lovers) elements.
Despite Aflora's opinions on the matter, there will
definitely be biting. Shadow, aka Shade, guarantees it.
This book ends on a cliffhanger.

You met Gina in Elemental Fae Academy. Find out what she's really up to in Fortune Fae Academy...

I never asked to be an Omega.

I'm a Fortune Fae—I see the future. But I didn't see this coming.

My Alpha will stop at nothing to possess me and has dragged me all the way to Fortune Fae Academy to join the other wide-eyed Omegas-in-training. He believes I'll survive--and I hope he's right.

He also believes I'll kneel at his feet.
He couldn't be more wrong about that.

I don't need three broody Betas and an asshat Alpha

telling me what to do. When I graduate the Academy as an ascended Omega, I'm rejecting my mate-circle and getting the hell out of here.

Except there's one slight problem. My Alpha has seen the future too... and he knows something I don't.

Whatever he thinks is going to happen, his cruel smirk says I'm not going anywhere.

Fortune Fae Academy is Book 1 in a Reverse Harem Omegaverse Romance. Be warned there are obsessive males who will stop at nothing to claim their fated mate. As this is a series, book 1 ends on a cliffhanger.

LEXI C FOSS

USA Today Bestselling Author Lexi C. Foss loves to play in dark worlds, especially the ones that bite. She lives in North Carolina with her husband and their furry children. When not writing, she's busy crossing items off her travel bucket list, or chasing eclipses around the globe. She's quirky, consumes way too much coffee, and loves to swim.

Want access to the most up-to-date information for all of Lexi's books? Sign-up for her newsletter here.

Lexi also likes to hang out with readers on Facebook in her exclusive readers group - Join Here.

Where To Find Lexi:
www.LexiCFoss.com

ALSO BY LEXI C. FOSS

Blood Alliance Series - Dystopian Paranormal

Chastely Bitten

Royally Bitten

Regally Bitten

Rebel Bitten

Kingly Bitten

Cruelly Bitten

Dark Provenance Series - Paranormal Romance

Heiress of Bael (FREE!)

Daughter of Death

Son of Chaos

Paramour of Sin

Princess of Bael

Elemental Fae Academy - Reverse Harem

Book One

Book Two

Book Three

Elemental Fae Queen

Winter Fae Queen

Hell Fae - Reverse Harem

Hell Fae Captive

Immortal Curse Series - Paranormal Romance

Book One: Blood Laws

Book Two: Forbidden Bonds

Book Three: Blood Heart

Book Four: Blood Bonds

Book Five: Angel Bonds

Book Six: Blood Seeker

Book Seven: Wicked Bonds

Immortal Curse World - Short Stories & Bonus Fun

Elder Bonds

Blood Burden

Mershano Empire Series - Contemporary Romance

Book One: The Prince's Game

Book Two: The Charmer's Gambit

Book Three: The Rebel's Redemption

Midnight Fae Academy - Reverse Harem

Ella's Masquerade

Book One

Book Two

Book Three

Book Four

Noir Reformatory - Ménage Paranormal Romance

The Beginning

First Offense

Second Offense

Underworld Royals Series - Dark Paranormal Romance

Happily Ever Crowned

Happily Ever Bitten

X-Clan Series - Dystopian Paranormal

Andorra Sector

X-Clan: The Experiment

Winter's Arrow

Bariloche Sector

Hunted

V-Clan Series - Dystopian Paranormal

Blood Sector

Vampire Dynasty - Dark Paranormal

Violet Slays

Sapphire Slays

Crossed Fates

Other Books

Scarlet Mark - Standalone Romantic Suspense

Rotanev - Standalone Poseidon Tale

Carnage Island - Standalone Reverse Harem Romance

About J.R. Thorn

J.R. Thorn is a Reverse Harem Paranormal Romance Author.

Subscribe to the J.R. Thorn Mailing List to be Notified of New Releases and Deals!

Addicted to Academy? Read more RH Academy by J.R. Thorn: Fortune Academy

Welcome to Fortune Academy, a school where supernaturals can feel at home—except, I have no idea what the hell I am.

ALSO BY J.R. THORN

All Books are Standalone Series listed by their sequential order of events

Elemental Fae Universe Reading List

Elemental Fae Academy: Books 1-3 (Co-Authored)

Midnight Fae Academy (Lexi C. Foss)

Fortune Fae Academy (J.R. Thorn)

Fortune Fae M/M Steamy Episodes (J.R. Thorn)

Blood Stone Series Universe Reading List

Seven Sins: The Blood Stone Series

- *Book 1: Succubus Sins*

- *Book 2: Siren Sins*

- *Book 3: Vampire Sins*

The Vampire Curse: Royal Covens

- *Book 1: Captivated*

- *Book 2: Compelled*

- *Book 3: Consumed*

Fortune Academy (Part I)

- *Year One*

- *Year Two*

- *Year Three*

Fortune Academy Underworld (Part II)

- *Episode 1: Burn in Hell*

- *Book Four*

- *Book Five (Coming Soon)*

- *Book Six (Coming Soon)*

Non-RH Books (J.R. Thorn writing as Jennifer Thorn)

Noir Reformatory Universe Reading List

Noir Reformatory: The Beginning

Noir Reformatory: First Offense

Sins of the Fae King Universe Reading List

Captured by the Fae King

Learn More at www.AuthorJRThorn.com